CW01507777

C

A Walk in the Woods

A Walk in the Woods
and other short stories

Including

Phil the Bath
Pig Tales
The Boy in the Picture
Strange Adventures
and more
Even Stranger Yarns

Graham Watkins
©2020

ISBN-13: 9798663340120

1 The Feud

It began on show day when pensioner Arnold Hopkins, a little man with an inflated opinion of himself, won a prize. Arnold who regarded the village show as an amusing nonsense wasn't expecting to win a prize and had only gone to the show because his wife insisted. He had no interest in cake competitions, flower arranging and the very idea of growing three identical runner beans was absurd.

'Well I never,' said his wife. 'You didn't tell me.'

A big red card and a 'First Rosette' had caught her attention. Arnold, who was short sighted, bent down and read the words. *Mr A. Hopkins, First Prize, Class Agricultural, Awarded for the Longest Bramble, Nine feet Eleven inches, a New Show Record.*

Arnold frowned at his wife. 'I need a drink.'

Drinkers in the beer tent queued to tease Arnold.

'Didn't know you were a bramble expert,' sniggered one.

'You should write to Blackberry Weekly. It might be a world record.'

Arnold blushed. 'It wasn't me,' he cried.

'The Guinness Book of Records should be told. You'll be famous.'

'What's your secret? asked another. 'Is it Baby Bio?'

'No. He sings to them.'

'What, like Lee Marvin?'

'That was trees.'

The more Arnold denied the bramble was his the worse the teasing got until he could stand no more. Arnold pulled himself up to his full five foot two inches, finished his beer with a pompous flourish, scowled at everyone and stomped from the beer tent pursued by laughter and more jibes.

'Are blackberries a profitable crop Arnold?'

'Do you get a government jam subsidy?'

'Well I never,' said Arnold and wondered who had impersonated him to play such a cruel trick. It could only be one man, his neighbour, that nasty clown, Joseph Williams. It had to be Joe.

Joe denied it of course. He smirked and said he'd had nothing to do with such a heinous crime but Arnold was convinced Joe was the villain who'd embarrassed him so. He'd disliked Joe ever since Christmas when the miserable sod had accused him of putting empty wine bottles in Joe's wheelie bin.

Arnold feigned ignorance of the bottles but didn't see what the fuss was about. He'd only put twelve bottles in. So what if the bin man refused to take them. It wasn't a big deal.

Now, after this latest embarrassing episode, Arnold hated Joe. The humiliation of the longest bramble was a declaration of war and Arnold knew he had to retaliate. Honour demanded it.

The following morning Joe discovered a neat pile of brown earth on the bonnet of his car.

'Moles,' called Arnold from across the road. 'Nasty little things. They tunnel through anything these days. I can lend you a trap if you like.'

Joe cursed Arnold. He was particularly proud of his car and polished it religiously every Sunday.

Arnold watched through his kitchen window and smiled as Joe carefully removed the earth with a dustpan and brush, and buffed the paintwork until it gleamed again.

A week later, Arnold noticed a sticker on the back of his car. So that was why passing motorists had honked and waved as he drove, and why some strange woman called him a Trumpian gun-toting redneck in the supermarket car park. But it didn't explain why a man had told him Bean was guilty.

I support Donald J Trump Make America Great Again said the sticker in bright red letters. Arnold fumed as he scraped it off. Bits of paint were coming away with the glue, damaging his car; Joe had gone too far this time.

Later when Arnold went to fill the car with petrol he found a second even bigger sticker on the back wing proclaiming *Mr Bean is innocent.*

Arnold had no idea why Mr Bean was innocent or even what crime he'd been accused of but there was one thing he did know; Joe would live to regret the day he vandalised the car.

'You're being childish,' said Arnold's wife and picked up her knitting. 'Two grown men. Really!'

'He started it,' said Arnold.

'Well I never,' said his wife.

'Click clack,' went the needles.

Early next morning Arnold crept across the road and glued a fifty pence coin to the pavement outside

Joe's house. He knew Joe always went to the shop and bought a newspaper before breakfast. At eight o'clock Joe emerged and walked down the drive. He stopped, stretched his arms and, as he did so, Arnold grabbed his phone and started to film. This was going to look good on Facebook. Joe would be a laughing stock.

But, instead of bending down and trying to pick up the coin, Joe waved casually at Arnold, made a rude sign, pointed at the money, shrugged and sauntered off along the pavement.

Disappointed he'd been rumbled, Arnold looked for another way to get his revenge and decided it had to be a more extreme reply, a final act to settle the matter; a bomb, yes that was the answer. Arnold would send Joe a bomb but there was a problem. How could he send a bomb without getting found out? Plus there was something else that made his idea improbable. Arnold didn't know how to make a bomb.

The answer came to Arnold as he was peeling potatoes. He'd put out a contract. Arnold had seen how it was done in gangster film. A hit they called it. Arnold didn't know if any hit men lived locally and, even if one did, using him or her - lady hit men seemed more popular these days - would be very risky. Arnold believed in supporting local businesses but not this time. Not when it involved explosives. No. The hit man needed to come from somewhere else, from as far away as possible. America seemed to be a good place to start looking because, as Arnold reasoned, lots of gangsters lived in America and it should be easy to find one. That was what Google was for; finding things and that is where he looked.

Of course sending Joe a real bomb was out of the question. Arnold didn't want to kill or actually hurt Joe and Arnold knew it was against the law to post letter bombs unless it was a bomb that would never explode.

Twenty dollars, said the website, *and the bomb will be delivered anonymously. Your victim will never know you ordered the hit.*

It was excellent value, an offer, as Don Corelone might have said, Arnold couldn't refuse. Arnold paid the twenty dollars by credit card completed his details, added the name of the target and the delivery address. As he selected United Kingdom from the drop down box a pop up window opened. *United Kingdom delivery by air mail is ten dollars extra. To complete your order click here.*

'What a cheek,' muttered Arnold and clicked.

Another pop up opened, *Special offer. For just five dollars your bomb will be signed for on delivery by the target. You're guaranteed satisfaction the contract is closed. To complete your order click here.*

'Closed?' said Arnold and clicked, no thanks.

Do you have other targets? asked the website. *Save money. Sign up for our multi blast, mega bomb, super deal.*

No, clicked Arnold.

Are you sure? This is a one in a lifetime explosive offer.

'YES,' shouted Arnold and clicked.

Recommend a friend and earn five dollars.

'NO. I don't want to,' shouted Arnold and clicked.

Order completed, said the website. *A confirmation email is on its way. Please check your spam folder. Thank you for ordering from Bomb by Post.*

Days later the postman pushed a padded envelope through Joe's letterbox. It was a tight fit and got stuck in the door. Joe pulled it out, read his name, saw the American postmark and wondered why someone he didn't know in North Carolina had sent him a strange lumpy letter. Joe took the letter into the living room, picked up a paperknife and inserted it.

Suddenly, the letter disintegrated, with a pop, covering the entire room in a fine layer of glitter dust.

Glitter was everywhere, in the curtains, the carpet, down the back of the settee, in his crystal glass cabinet, in Joe's hair and even in the turn-ups of his trousers. It took Joe days to clear up the mess.

As he vacuumed behind the television he found scraps of envelope, a spring and a plastic card with writing on it. *Do you have an enemy?* it asked. *Bomb by Post is what you need. We have a great selection, glitter, stink, paint, klaxon... Check out our website at....*

Joe logged on, selected a klaxon, perma stink combination; an ear busting blast followed by a foul eggy smell guaranteed to linger for months, on special offer and pressed buy.

Do you have other targets? asked the website. *Save money. Sign up for our multi blast, mega bomb, super deal.*

No, clicked Joe.

Are you sure? This is a one in a lifetime explosive offer.

Joe clicked complete order.

Recommend a friend and earn five dollars.

'No thank you,' said Joe and clicked send.

Order completed, said the website. *A confirmation email is on its way. Please check your spam folder. Thank you for ordering from Bomb by Post.*

Arnold never received Joe's stink bomb. It triggered in the hold of a Boeing 747 at thirty thousand feet. Economy class passengers at the back of the plane heard a strange distant hooter and were the first to notice the rancid smell. It spread slowly forward, through the plane, asphyxiating passengers. Opening air vents made things worse, blasting foul air into the cabin. There was, no relief; no windows to open, nowhere to hide. By the time it reached the first class cabin oxygen masks had been deployed. The captain diverted and made an emergency landing in Greenland. Passengers, scrambling to get away from the stench, evacuated down escape-slides. They stood on the tarmac, eyes watering, coughing and gasping in the cold arctic air.

Because it was never delivered Joe heard nothing from Arnold about the stink bomb. 'I've had the last laugh,' he chuckled to himself. 'Taught the old codger a lesson he won't forget.'

Which is exactly what Arnold thought, when he heard no more from Joe. Although the two men never spoke of it, the feud was over.

2 ☐ A Day Out

'Let's go for a walk tomorrow.' It wasn't warm in the lounge but those words spoken by Alice were enough to make Hugh sweat. He knew what they meant. His wife didn't do strolls in the park. An Alice walk was an expedition into the unknown, a serious exercise, an iron-man endurance test. It involved meticulous planning and research followed by hours of tramping through the countryside.

Hugh remembered their last walk, the sleet, the biting wind and the farm gate, under two feet of water. 'There's no way around. We must go back,' he'd said.

'No,' said Alice and marched through the icy water.

Hugh followed as he always did, sinking to his knees in slime, feeling cold mud seeping between his toes.

Alice had called him a moaner as they'd sheltered in the church porch, wrung their socks out and eaten soggy sandwiches.

'A cliff walk. Cemaes Head,' announced Alice and turned on her laptop.

'It's going to rain tomorrow,' said Hugh.

Alice pointed to the map on the screen. 'We'll start here. There's a bridleway where Honey can run free.'

Honey sat up and wagged her tail.

'You know don't you? Clever Girl. She knows Hugh. Be a dear. Fish-paste and cucumber, would you Hugh?'

Hugh went to the kitchen and opened the bread-bin, leaving Alice to plot the route and download it to the sat-nav. He'd bought the sat-nav for her birthday after they got lost in the Berwyn Mountains. The memory of that walk, searching for the Land of the Dead in a storm, still haunted him.

'Twenty kilometres,' declared Alice as he returned to the lounge. 'Did you make the sandwiches? We'll start early.'

The following morning was bright and sunny, full of promise as they drove to Cemaes Head. Hugh parked where Alice told him and they put on their walking boots while Honey bounced about in the back of the car. Hugh pulled on the rucksack containing their lunch and the two large water bottles Alice always insisted on.

'They balance the rucksack,' she explained, 'and you never know when you might need them.'

'We never drink it,' muttered Hugh. 'I'm lugging a gallon of water twelve miles for nothing.'

'I think we're ready. Hugh, get Honey out of the car.' Alice switched on the sat-nav and waited for it to orientate.

It beeped.

'The bridleway is over there. Five hundred metres and then we turn left onto a footpath heading east.'

They started along the bridleway with Alice and Honey walking quickly followed by Hugh. Behind them, the estuary reflected the deep blue cloudless sky.

Hugh was puffing by the time they reached the stile leading to the footpath. The bottles in his rucksack weighed heavy and were digging into his back. Beads of cold perspiration ran down the inside of his shirt.

'Hugh, there's no dog gate,' said Alice and handed him the lead. 'You're going to have to carry Honey over the stile.'

Hugh stared at the fifty pound retriever and the rickety wooden stile.

Alice clambered over the stile and, with a little jump, land safely in the field. 'Come on Hugh. We haven't got all day.'

Honey, eager to continue, was up with her front paws on the stile.

Hugh leant down to pick her up and, propelled by the inertia of his backpack, fell forward landing on the dog. He tried again, moving more slowly and managed to get his arms around her tummy. Lifting Honey he climbed on to the first step. The next, however, presented a problem. Its narrow wooden plank was higher than he expected and, with both hands entangled with Honey, Hugh had no way of hanging on. Worse still, there was nothing to hang on to. Hugh took a deep breath and up he went.

Honey wriggled. The plank wobbled and Hugh found himself in mid air. He shrieked, let go of Honey and landed with a loud pop on his back.

13

Alice bent over him. 'You didn't have to jump off the stile. Are you all right?'

'No I'm not,' said Hugh angrily and got up. 'My back's all wet. I think one of your bottle's burst.'

'My bottles!' Alice giggled. 'Look at your trousers. You look like you've wet yourself.'

Honey scampered around Hugh wagging her tail.

'You'll soon dry,' said Alice. She checked the sat-nav and, summoning Honey, set off for the next waypoint; a farmyard half a mile away.

Hugh followed, waddling like John Wayne, with cold water running down his legs.

As they approached the farmyard, two sheepdogs appeared, barking aggressively.

A shabbily dressed farmer wearing a flat cap and muddy wellingtons walked towards them. 'Russ, Bruno, QUIET.'

The dogs snarled a final warning and backed away.

'Wad' you want?' demanded the farmer. He looked quizzically at Hugh's wet trousers.

'We're doing a walk out to the cliff and back to the estuary,' explained Alice cheerfully.

'You ain't' coming this way. It's private.'

'No it isn't. It's a public footpath.' Alice showed him the GPS.

'That's a fancy thing but it ain't' no good. You'll have to go back to the road. Footpath's closed.'

'Closed. How can it be closed?' demanded Alice.

'I closed it.'

You can't. It's a public right of way,' said Alice firmly.

'Well I have,' said the farmer equally firmly.

'Maybe we should go back,' said Hugh.

'Shut up Hugh. Now look here. you can't close it.'

'I ain't' cut the field. Don't want no hikers trampling my hay.'

'Don't worry. We'll walk around the edge of your field. Your hay will be fine.' Alice smiled reassuringly.

The farmer lifted his cap and scratched his brow. 'That's as maybe but I'm telling you, the path's still closed.'

'Why?' Alice was angry. 'Give me one good reason why we shouldn't go that way.'

'The bull.' replied the farmer, 'in the next field.'

'This isn't a good idea,' said Hugh.

'We're not going back, Hugh. Everyone knows you can't put a bull in a field where there's a footpath. It's against the law. Come along Hugh.' Alice pushed past the farmer and marched on.

The farmer replaced his cap firmly on his head and scowled at Hugh.

Hugh smiled apologetically, shrugged and hurried after Alice.

The first field was as the farmer had claimed; chest high hay ready to be cut. Alice and Hugh followed a stone wall around to the far side of the field where the wall was higher than a man, a wide ladder stile led to the next field.

Walking in the warm sunshine, beside the wall, Hugh's trousers had started to dry and, encouraged by Alice that the farmer's talk of a bull was well 'all bull', he was starting to feel better.

The stile, a wide solid affair with eight steps leading to the top, beckoned.

'Up you go Hugh,' ordered Alice, 'and have a look. I bet there's no bull.'

Hugh climbed up and peered over the top of the wall. Ahead, about five hundred metres away, he could see the next wall and a metal gate. It would be a steady uphill walk across lush pasture.

Alice's voice drifted up from behind. 'Any sign of a bull?'

'No. There aren't any animals at all.'

Alice clambered up beside him. 'What did I tell you?'

Not wanting to be left behind, Honey followed and the three of them surveyed the field.

Alice was first to climb over. She bent down and unclipped Honey's lead. 'Come on Hugh,' she called, striding away.

Now Honey was off the lead and wanting to explore. She was out of sight by the time Hugh climbed down.

They were half way across the field when there was a distant bark followed by silence. Honey appeared, running towards Hugh and hot on her heels a large white monster; two thousand pounds of testosterone; the largest bull Hugh had ever seen. 'Run,' he shouted. He needn't have bothered.

Alice was already sprinting towards the gate in the distance.

Hugh was still fifty metres from safety when Honey overtook him. Any moment he expected the thunder of hooves, to feel the bull's hot breath on his neck, to be trampled underfoot.

'Come on Hugh,' shouted Alice from the far side of the gate.

Hugh glanced over his shoulder, missed a step, stumbled and landed in a squidgy cow pat. Exhausted he waited, with his eyes tight shut, for the inevitable...

Nothing happened. There was no thunder of hooves, no hot breath or trampling underfoot.

He opened them and saw the bull. It had lost interest in the trespassers to its field and was ambling away.

Hugh stood up, wiped cow dung from his cheeks, and joined Alice.

'I told you the water would be useful,' said Alice as she rinsed his face. She consulted the sat-nav. 'We need to walk west for point five of a kilometre.' And off they went again. An hour passed. They stopped. 'That's odd,' said Alice. 'How far would you say we've walked?'

'I dunno' an hour; must be a couple of kilometres at least.'

'Look,' said Alice and handed the sat-nav to Hugh. 'It says we've only walked 200metres.'

Hugh took the sat-nav and examined it. He snorted. 'It wasn't point five of a kilometre it was five kilometres. There's a spot of smut on the screen.' He passed the sat-nav back to Alice.

She wiped the screen. 'So we have to walk west another three kilometres. Let's finish this section and it will be time for lunch.'

Five minutes later they'd crossed the next field and reached the cliff edge.

'What now?' said Hugh. 'Do we keep walking west, across the sea? Do you know where we are?'

'Shut up Hugh.' Alice pressed a button on the sat-nav and shook it. 'It's stopped working.'

'Probably doesn't like the sea.'

'Don't be stupid. You try,' snapped Alice and thrust the sat-nav at Hugh.

'Batteries.'

'What?' said Alice.

'You did bring spare batteries.'

Alice shook her head.

'Pass me the map.'

'It's in the car,' said Alice. 'Didn't think we'd need it, not with the sat-nav.'

Hugh rolled his eyes, Honey wagged her tail.

'You're the great navigator. It's your walk,' said Hugh. 'Which way?'

'Don't get on at me.' Alice looked both ways along the cliff. 'You think it's all my fault. How was I to know the sat-nav was wrong?' She sniffed.

'It wasn't wrong Alice. You put a waypoint in the middle of the sea and didn't READ THE THING PROPERLY.'

'Don't shout at me.'

'I'M NOT shouting.'

They stood glaring at each other, Alice embarrassed by her silly mistakes and surprised at

18

Hugh's sudden uncharacteristic outburst. At the same time Hugh was feeling rather pleased with himself.

Then Hugh noticed something was wrong. 'Where's Honey?'

Honey had slipped her lead and was trotting away along the cliff path.

'Oh no,' said Alice and ran after the dog, closely followed by Hugh. They caught up with Honey at a kissing gate and put her back on the lead. Next to the gate was a bench seat. They sat down to catch their breath.

A strange moaning sound wafted on the sea breeze. Honey's ears pricked up. She strained pulling towards the cliff edge. Hugh got up and moved forward. He looked down to the rocks below. 'Come and look. There are seals on the beach and there are some pups.'

Alice joined him. 'The big ones look like huge slugs that have crawled up onto the beach.'

The three of them stood watching and listening as the seals called to each other.

'Isn't the sea beautiful?' said Hugh.

'Let's have lunch,' said Alice.

They sat back down. Alice was unwrapping her sandwiches when Honey's head shoved its way under her arm. Their eyes met.

'Are you hungry?' Alice gave a sandwich to the dog. It vanished in one gulp.

'Give me more,' said Honey's eyes.

'You shouldn't do that,' said Hugh.

'Hugh, don't be so heartless. She's hungry.'

19

A seagull landed in front of them. Honey growled but the bird stood its ground eyeing the food.

'Get away,' yelled Alice and waved her arms. The seagull squawked, lifted off and flew close over Alice's head emptying its bowel as it went.

'Oh God! The bloody thing's shit on me,' shrieked Alice wiping her sodden hair. 'It stinks of fish. Hugh, do something.'

Hugh rewrapped his fishpaste and cucumber sandwich told Alice to learn forward and emptied the last of the water over Alice's head. He produced a wet wipe from the rucksack and wiped her hair. 'It's the best I can do,' he said screwing up the wet wipe and poking it into the empty bottle. 'Probably likes fishpaste.'

'What?' said Alice.

'The seagull. I said it probably likes fishpaste.'

Alice stood up. 'I'm not staying here. It might come back. Come on Honey.'

They followed the cliff path, around the headland and were returning towards the estuary when Honey stopped and refused to move.

Alice pulled the lead but the dog wouldn't budge or move no matter how much Alice coaxed or tugged. It was if she her paws has been riveted to the footpath.

Then Honey howled like a stricken banshee, started to pant and fell over, straddling the footpath like a lumpy fur rug.

Alice cradled Honey's head. 'Look at her eyes Hugh. They've disappeared into the back of her

20

head and her tongue's just hanging there. Do something.'

Hugh looked at the dog and at his distraught wife. 'I told you not to give her the fish-paste.' He bent down and tried to coax Honey up. 'Come on girl. Up you get.'

Honey didn't move.

'Give me the water Hugh, quickly.'

'I can't. It's all gone.'

'I think she's dying. What are we going to do?' shrieked Alice.

Hugh scanned the cliff path hoping to see a hiker, someone, anyone who might help. There wasn't a soul in sight.

'I can't carry her. What do you want me to do?'

'Hugh, I've poisoned her. I know I have. I'm sorry Honey.' Alice lifted Honey's head and tried to push her limp tongue back into her mouth. It slipped from Alice's hand and lay across her knee. 'Use your phone,' shrieked Alice. 'Call the air ambulance.'

'For a dog? It's for people not for sick dogs,' said Hugh. 'You stay here with her. I'll get help.'

Alice watched him jog away along the path and vanish from sight. She sobbed. Why had she been so stupid and got them lost? Why had she poisoned her lovely Honey? Hugh had been right. She should have listened to him. What have I done? She stroked Honey's head and wept. 'I'm sorry Honey. I'm so sorry.'

Hugh jogged for nearly half an hour to reach help stopping only to climb each stile and catch his breath. Honey's life depended on him. Alice would never forgive him if he failed. He couldn't give up. He just couldn't.

Mrs Evans was mucking out a horsebox when a very bothered looking middle aged man, clutching his side, appeared in her farmyard. 'Are you all right?' she called.

'I've got a stitch,' replied Hugh and bent double with his hands on his knees. 'Do you have any water?' he hissed.

Mrs Evans fetched a jug of water and listened to Hugh's garbled tale, punctuated by gasps for air and gulps of water. Then, without any hesitation, she tipped the muck from her wheelbarrow. 'Here,' she said. 'Take this.'

The climb back to the top of the cliff was torture. Hugh's legs felt like lead. His lungs were on fire. His arms ached and the wheelbarrow made everything worse. Somehow he had to hoist the unwieldy barrow over stile after stile and the metal monster got heavier with every step. 'I can't give up,' he repeated, again and again, mantra like, until the effort of speaking overwhelmed him but still he went on pushing one weary foot in front of the other.

Alice, red faced and tearful, saw him staggering towards her.

Hugh collapsed, on his back, beside Honey. 'Give me a minute,' he croaked and stared up at the endless blue sky.

22

Alice knew she had to do something. She tried to lift Honey into the barrow. She'd managed to get the dog's front legs into the barrow when it suddenly slid sideways and tipped spilling Honey. Alice lost her balance, let go of Honey, and landed with a thump on her bottom. It was the final blow. She could take no more and there the three of them lay - a frozen cliff top tableau of disaster and despair.

The sun was lower in the sky when Hugh stirred. He encouraged Alice and, between them, they managed to lift Honey into the wheelbarrow. Everything was fine until they reached the first stile. They stopped, looked at the wheelbarrow and knew it was the end of the walk. Lifting Honey and the wheelbarrow over was a Herculean task, far beyond them.

Hugh and Alice sat on the grass and looked towards the setting sun.

'I wish we had some water,' said Alice.'I'm parched.'

'We should have started with an extra bottle,' said Hugh.

'I'm sorry Hugh.'

'What for?'

'For everything.' Alice sniffed and wiped her nose. 'Honey didn't deserve to die like that; poisoned by a fishpaste sandwich.'

'Funny way to walk a dog,' said a jovial voice. Leaning over the stile was a young man and beside him stood Mrs Evans.

'This is Barry, my son,' said Mrs Evans. 'I was worried. We've come to see if you need any help.'

'We're not walking her,' said Alice and shook her head.

'I'm sorry,' said Barry. 'I didn't mean to be flippant.'

With four to help, the barrow and poor Honey was carried down to the farm. They left the wheelbarrow in the yard and went into the house where Mrs Evans made some tea. It was a sombre meal. 'What are you going to do with your dog?' she asked.

Hugh put his cup down and looked at Alice. 'We'll take her home and bury her in the garden.'

When they'd finished tea, Barry drove Hugh to collect his car. Driving back into the farmyard Hugh was surprised to see Alice kneeling on the cobbles. Beside her stood Mrs Evans and between them sat Honey.

'She's alive Hugh,' shouted Alice.

'What happened?' asked Hugh as he hurried across the yard.

'I needed the barrow,' said Mrs Evans, 'for the horses. When I went to lift her out I could feel her tummy rumbling so I put her down gently and saw she was breathing.'

Alice squeezed Honey lovingly. 'Thank goodness. She's drunk a gallon of water.' She hugged her again which caused an unfortunate reaction. Honey made a strange gurgling noise, retched and up came a gallon of water followed by what looked like the remnants of a sandwich.

'What's that stink?' asked Mrs Evans. 'Smells like fish.'

Alice pulled a face. 'I dunno'.' She looked at Hugh.

'She must have eaten something,' said Hugh.

'How is she?' asked Hugh as they were driving home.

'She's asleep on the back seat,' said Alice. 'Hugh, do you like fishpaste?'

'Not really.'

'Why didn't you say?'

Hugh shrugged. 'Why didn't you ask?'

A Walk in the Woods

3 **Mushrooms**

'Mushrooms,' said Mrs Wilson. 'It's a kit, just turned up on the front door step.' She pointed at the brown cardboard box at the end of the kitchen table. 'I'm going to grow them.' She poured two cups of Jamaica Blue Mountain from the coffee maker on the Aga, placed the cups on saucers and handed one to her new neighbour. She looked at the girl; at her ill fitting t-shirt, torn jeans, the gothic tattoos of skulls, chains and flowers covering both arms. Mrs Wilson smiled politely, wiped a drip from the spout of the percolator, returned it to the stove and opened a cake tin.

'You must try this,' she said offering the girl a slice of cake. 'I made it yesterday.'

Rhian took a slice, cupped her hand underneath it and bit into the soft sponge. 'Ta,' she spluttered sending crumbs flying. 'Lovely.' She wiped chocolate icing from her face with her hand.

Mrs Wilson passed a plate across the table and watched the girl devour the cake. She took a second slice.

'So the council gave you the upstairs flat,' said Mrs Wilson. 'What sort of state is it in?'

'It's a dump. The walls are mouldy. There's just a bed, a chair and a poxy two ring cooker in the kitchen.'

'You're very lucky to get a flat.'

'The woman at the social told me that. She said it was because I deserved a new start.' Rhian pushed the plate away and looked around.

'A new start?'

'Your 'ouse is lovely. So warm. You bin 'ere long?'

'Thirty seven years. Jack and I moved here in 1982. We were some of the first tenants on the estate. Before they split some of the houses into upstairs and downstairs flats. Spoilt the estate. It was nice before then. Young families. We all got on together. Not like today. No one speaks. I hardly see anyone these days.'

'Jack? 'e your 'usband?'

Mrs Wilson nodded. 'He died two years ago last week... Yes. Well.' She stood up and collected the plates and cups together.

'Oh. Sorry.' Rhian looked around... 'You got any kids Mrs Wilson?'

'Two. One's in America the other in Japan. He works for the government,' said Mrs Wilson proudly. 'And I've got five grandchildren.'

'Nice. Did ya buy it?'

'Buy what?'

The mushroom kit.'

'No,' said Mrs Wilson. 'It just turned up. The label was addressed to a Mr H. Potter at my address. H. Potter doesn't live here so I rang the Flying Mushroom Company.'

'Who?'

'The Flying Mushroom Company, where the mushrooms came from. They told me there'd been a mistake.'

'Wot sort of mistake?'

'The man wouldn't say. He just said he'd send a new box to Mr Potter and to forget it. He sounded a bit creepy. I asked him what to do with the mushroom kit and he said he didn't want it back, to throw it away. Then he hung up.'

They sat looking at the box.

'How do ya grow mushrooms?'

'I don't know. It can't be that hard,' replied Mrs Wilson, loading the dishwasher. 'There are some instructions in the box.'

The phone in Rhian's pocket buzzed. She glanced at the screen, tapped it with her thumb and got up. 'I gotta go. Ta for the cake.'

Rhian returned to Mrs Wilson's two days later and saw the cardboard box was gone. In its place sat a plastic bag filled with what looked like rubbish.

'It's a mixture of straw and coffee grounds,' explained Mrs Wilson, 'for the mycelium to eat.'

Rhian put down her coffee cup. 'My silly what?'

'Mycelium, it's what mushrooms grow out from. Says here, it's their roots.' She pointed at the instructions.

'Oh...' Rhian fiddled with her sleeve. 'Guess what? A man from the council delivered a fridge yesterday and a washing machine. 'e said if I ask right they'll give me a microwave and a telly.'

'For nothing?'

'Yeah. I ain't got no money.'

'Mrs Wilson fussed with her apron, folding it carefully and putting it away. 'Well, it all seems very strange to me. You getting all there appliances

29

and not having to pay for them.' She turned and looked at Rhian. 'Are you going to get a job?'

'A job! Yeah. I've been looking.'

'Really? What sort of job have you been looking for?'

Rhian got her phone out and studied the screen. ''ave a look.' She handed the phone to Mrs Wilson.

'What is it?' asked Mrs Wilson peering at the screen. 'The writing's tiny. I can't read it.'

'It's a CD. The woman in the job centre said I 'ad to 'ave one to get a job. I've been writing it.'

Mrs Wilson squinted at the screen. 'You mean a CV, a curriculum vitae.'

'Yeah, a curriclum thing. I'm getting a job. I'm going to be an entrepreneur.'

'An entrepreneur. It's a long word. Do you know what that means?' Mrs Wilson smiled and handed back the phone. 'So you want to work for yourself.'

'It's better than working in a poxy shop. An' I'll make decent money.' Rhian pushed the phone back in her pocket and looked at the cake tin. 'Mrs Wilson, I bet your grandkids love your chocolate cake.'

Mrs Wilson opened the tin and cut Rhian a slice. She replaced the lid. 'They've never tasted my cakes. None of them have ever been here. They didn't even come to Jack's funeral.'

'Do you visit them, then?'

'Go on an aeroplane, me, at my age?' Mrs Wilson frowned. 'No. They don't want to see a silly old woman like me.'

A week later the plastic bag was filled with white gossamer strands of fungus. 'That's the mycelium,' said Mrs Wilson. 'It's almost ready to fruit.'

'To fruit?' Rhian watched Mrs Wilson open the top of the bag and point to the tiny shoots.

'See, tiny mushrooms. They'll be ready to harvest in a few days,' said Mrs Wilson. She picked up a small water bottle and sprayed a mist on the contents.

'Wot you goin' to do with them?'

'I'm going to cook them. You can help me eat them if you like.' She folded the top of the bag over. 'How's your job hunting going?'

'Nuffin yet,' Rhian looked disappointed. 'I went to an interview at the Castle Hotel yesterday to be an entrepreneur, like I said.'

'That's good. How did the interview go?'

'There was a load of us in this big room. The woman doing the interview stood at the front, wiv a microphone and said we was all goin' to be rich. All we had to do was buy some stock to sell.'

Mrs Wilson sat down opposite Rhian. 'What sort of stock?'

'Cleanin' stuff. Three 'undred and fifty poxy quid's worth of cleanin' stuff. She said all we had to do was sell it and we'd have over seven hundred quids profit in our pockets.'

'But you don't have three hundred and fifty pounds.' Mrs Wilson took hold of Rhian's hands. 'Have you had anything to eat today?'

Rhian pulled away and sat staring at her lap.

'I thought so.' Mrs Wilson collected bowls, went to the Aga and ladled soup into them. 'It's tomato I made it this morning.' She cut two hunks of bread and served Rhian. 'Eat, while it's still hot.'

They ate in silence.

'You're going to have to get a proper job,' announced Mrs Wilson as she cleared away. 'Forget all the entrepreneur nonsense. Something honest like in a shop or a pub. Anything that gets you started, earns you some money.'

'I've been trying, Mrs Wilson,' said Rhian tearfully. 'Honest.'

The following evening Mrs Wilson was dusting her front room when she heard a loud exhaust. A battered car cruised slowly along the road. Minutes later it returned and stopped. She watched a young man, scruffy looking, his head half shaved, half dreadlocks, wearing a black knee length coat get out, glance at a phone and look up and down the street. He thrust the phone in his pocket, walked along the path, up the steps to Rhian's flat and tapped on the door. It opened, he disappeared inside and the door shut.

It was late the next day when Rhian came around.

'Who was your visitor?' asked Mrs Wilson as she poured coffee.

'Wot visitor?'

'The man who called to see you last night.'

Rhian hesitated. 'You saw 'im then?'

'I couldn't fail to. His car woke me up at six o'clock this morning. Probably woke the whole street.'

'You won't tell the council Mrs Wilson will ya? Promise.'

'Tell the council, certainly not.' Mrs Wilson frowned. 'What sort of person do you thing I am?' She opened the cake tin and put two plates on the table. 'You need to be very careful young lady.'

They sat in undeclared silence each in their own thoughts a silence interrupted only by the rhythmic tick of the hall clock.

It was Mrs Wilson who broke the spell. 'Let's harvest the mushrooms.' She got up and opened the plastic bag at the end of the table. 'Aren't they lovely?'

They stood together looking at the mushrooms, a cluster of long stems, bluish at the bottom, sprouting from the mycelium, each stem supporting a conical yellowy-brown cap.

Rhian giggled. 'They look like nipples.' She pointed to the bump at the top of a cap.

'They do, don't they?' said Mrs Wilson and grinned. She took a sharp knife from the kitchen drawer, carefully cut the stems near the base and placed the harvest in a bowl.

'Come for lunch tomorrow; one o'clock. I'm going to cook something special for us,' said Mrs Wilson as Rhian was leaving.

Rhian opened the back door and hesitated. 'It was Gary... the man you saw...'

'Gary?'

'Are you cross with me?'

'No. Why should I be cross? It's none of my business. I'll see you tomorrow.'

That evening Mrs Wilson was busy baking. She didn't hear or see Gary return to Rhian's flat but his car woke her as he drove away the next morning. Although it was early, she got up, dressed and went downstairs. She felt the quiches she'd cooked the previous night. All four were cold. She wrapped three, in tin foil, put them in the freezer and added them to the stock list she kept taped to the inside of the cupboard door. The fourth she put in the fridge ready for lunch and, after breakfast, being Thursday, she cleaned upstairs.

By one o'clock she'd changed and laid the kitchen table for two. A mixed salad marinated with olive oil, salt and vinegar, sat in a wooden bowl in the centre of the table beside it a stainless bowl of sliced beetroot, another of potatoes in mayonnaise and one of mushrooms drizzled with lime juice, an idea she'd got from the little recipe book that came with the mushroom kit. Mrs Wilson surveyed the tableau and, after some thought, fetched two wine glasses from the cabinet in the front room together with the unopened bottle of Chardonnay from Christmas. She polished the glasses, set them down, put the wine in the fridge and waited.

The hall clock marked the minutes. 'Tick... Tick... Tick...' It stuck the quarter hour. Mrs Wilson wandered into the front room and peered through the window at Rhian's front door. It was shut. She returned to the kitchen and sat down. The half hour chimed.

Suddenly, Rhian burst through the door grinning like a fool. 'I've got a job. Mrs Wilson, I've done it. I've got a job.'

Rhian's news and her obvious excitement drove all thought of annoyance from Mrs Wilson's mind. The room came alive as Rhian explained and bounced around the kitchen. 'I was walkin' down the high street when I saw the sign.'

'What sign?'

'The one for the job.'

'What job?'

'In the window. Mr Pugh's window.'

'The greengrocer?'

'Yeah. I start on Saturday. On 'is market stall and in 'is shop. Eight quid an hour and it's cash in me 'and. He says I don't have to tell the social.'

Mrs Wilson listened, waiting until Rhian ran out of puff. 'That is good news.' She went to the fridge, opened the wine and poured two glasses. 'It calls for a celebration. To your new career and a new start in life.' She toasted Rhian and placed the chilled quiche on the table. 'Now, let's have some lunch. I've put some of the mushrooms in the quiche but you must try these.' She pointed to the bowl of mushrooms. They're soaked in lime juice.'

Rhian tried one and pulled a face. 'There a bit chewy and sharp. I'm not sure if I like them.'

They continued to eat. Rhian refilled the glasses.

'What does your boyfriend Gary do? Does he have a job?'

35

'Yeah, 'e's an apprentice plumber. Goes to college one day a week.'

Mrs Wilson was enjoying the conversation. It was good to have company. It was a long time since she'd shared a meal with someone; two years since Jack's death. She felt good, light headed, happy. Her cheeks felt warm. 'Oh my. This wine's strong,' she said suppressing a snigger.

'You alright, Mrs Wilson? Your face is very red.'

'I'm not used to wine. I'm a bit tiddly.' Mrs Wilson tried to stand up but her legs wouldn't move. She looked down at them and tried to decide if they were crossed or uncrossed. 'Are my legs crossed?' she asked.

'Wot?'

'Have a look. Are my legs crossed?'

Rhian bent down and looked under the table. 'One's crossed and the other isn't.' She sniggered, sat up and burst out laughing.

'That's stupid,' said Mrs Wilson. 'What's wrong with your face. It's wonky.' She leaned over. 'No. Still wonky.' Now, they were both laughing hysterically. The laughter and confusion continued. They'd stopped eating and just sat there pulling faces at each other.

'Did I tell you what Gary's 'obby is?' giggled Rhian.

'He's got a hobby. No.'

''e's a fillatist.'

'A flutist. He plays a flute?'

'No.' Tears were rolling down Rhian's face. 'A fillatist.'

'What does a fillatsit do?' roared Mrs Wilson.

'Stamps, 'e collects stamps.'

'You mean a philatelist.'

'Yeah. That's wot I said. A fillalltist,' declared Rhian resting her chin on the table.

'We'd better clear up,' sniggered Mrs Wilson and, after concentrating hard, managed to stand. She collected the dirty plates, opened the fridge door and shoved them in. 'There, that's done,' she declared slamming the door shut. 'Is there any more wine?' She sat down with a bump and peered at Rhian but it wasn't Rhian's face. 'Jack, what are you doing here?'

Mrs Wilson tried to focus, to be sure what she was seeing. She shut her eyes, shook her head and opened them again.

Jack was sitting across the table from her, smiling as if he knew something. 'Wine at lunchtime. That's not like you Betty. Are you celebrating? That's good. I don't like you being sad. You should celebrate more often. Get out of the house.' Jack leaned back in his chair. 'Your new friend is nice.'

'My new friend?' Mrs Wilson tried to understand what her dead husband was telling her.

'Rhian, that's her name isn't it? Seems like a nice girl...' Jack's voice was distant now, fading away.

'Don't go Jack,' whispered Mrs Wilson, 'there's so much to talk about.' But she was too late. Jack had gone replaced by a void in her heart that ached. 'I miss you so much,' she whimpered and put her head in her arms.

'Mrs Wilson, 'ow do ya feel?' The question came from somewhere distant. A far off place, remote, not part of the strange dream-like world where she was.

Mrs Wilson opened her eyes and found herself sprawled on the sofa in her front room. Rhian was standing over her. She sat up. 'What time is it?'

'Half past seven. You passed out. Here, I've made you a mug of tea.'

Mrs Wilson took the tea and sipped it gingerly. 'That's good. Was I drunk?'

'No. It wasn't the wine. You 'ad a trip, a psychedelic trip.'

'What? That's impossible. It was the wine. I'm not used to it.'

"ow's your 'ead?' asked Rhian. 'I bet you aint got an hangover.'

MrsWilson had to admit Rhian was right. There was no headache, no foul taste in her mouth. She didn't have a hangover in fact she felt good. No, better than good. She felt fantastic, happier than she'd felt for months, years even.

'Mushrooms Mrs Wilson. You've been growing magic mushrooms.' Rhian sat down beside Mrs Wilson. 'Good, wasn't it?' And there they sat, side by side, grinning like Cheshire Cats.

As Rhian was leaving, Mrs Wilson asked her to take the bag of mushroom spores out to the dustbin. 'It's for the best,' she said. But, instead to putting the mycelium in the bin, Rhian hurried up the stairs to her flat, checked that no one was looking, went

38

inside and hid the bag in a cupboard. She didn't see Mrs Wilson watching from the window.

The following morning, Mrs Wilson rang her son in Japan and left a message on his answer phone. Then she rang America and spoke to her daughter.

Rhian didn't visit Mrs Wilson the following week. 'It's her new job,' Mrs Wilson told herself. 'She must be busy.' One afternoon she heard Gary's car and looked through the frontroom window. Rhian and Gary were lugging some bags up the stairs to the flat. Gary returned to the car, took a large box from the boot and carried it indoors.

Mrs Wilson had baked a ginger cake that morning and had an idea. She cut two generous slices, put them on a plate, hurried outside, up the steps to Rhian's front door and knocked.

The door cracked open and Rhian's face appeared. 'Oh! 'ello Mrs Wilson.'

'I thought you might like some cake.' Mrs Wilson pushed the plate forward.

Rhian opened the door enough to take the plate and Mrs Wilson saw Gary was standing behind her.

'I'd ask you in but...' Rhian hesitated.

'The place is a mess,' said Gary.

'Yeah, a mess,' added Rhian. 'Ta for the cake. I'll bring the plate back,' she said and shut the door.

'How odd,' muttered Mrs Wilson as she trudged down the stairs.

That evening, she was watching television when there was a knock at the back door.

'I've brought your plate back,' said Rhian. 'I've washed it up.' She held the plate up. 'Sorry 'bout shutting the door but Gary said no one was allowed in 'cause of the mess.'

Mrs Wilson took the plate. 'Well, it wasn't very nice to have the door shut in my face,' she said frostily.

'Gary 'ad his stuff spread all over the floor. He was frightened you would tread on it.'

A car revved in the road. Rhian shuffled nervously. 'I've gotta go. Gary's taking me to the pictures.

In the days that followed Mrs Wilson noticed Rhian wasn't going to work. Not only that, but there was a steady stream of visitors to her flat. Strange men would appear, spend a few minutes there, sometimes not even going inside, and depart as quickly as they arrived. Rhian was civil enough when they spoke in the street but she rarely visited Mrs Wilson.

And then there was Gary. The boyfriend changed his car. Gone was the banger that belched blue smoke replaced with a tidy looking hatchback but what was he was up to coming and going with so many boxes?

Mrs Wilson however had other more pressing things to think about. She had also changed. She'd joined a bowls club and started to write short stories which she took to a writer's group that met in the library every Thursday. Despite being busier than ever she didn't forget the afternoon when Rhian came to lunch when they ate the mushrooms. She also remembered the bag of mushroom spores Rhian had taken back to her flat and a niggling thought began to fester in the back of her mind.

The morning of the police raid started with loud bangs and men shouting. Mrs Wilson glanced at the bedside clock; four am. Flashing blue lights filled the street. Men were running everywhere. She watched Rhian and Gary being pushed into a police car and driven away. Their flat door, smashed from its hinges, hung at a drunken angle. People in white boiler suits were carrying plastic bags from the flat.

By nine o'clock they had gone leaving a solitary policeman standing at the top of the stairs.

Mrs Wilson went outside with a slice of cake and a mug of tea. 'I thought you might be thirsty.'

The policeman, a new recruit fresh from college, took the mug and cupped it between his hands. He stamped his feet to keep the blood circulating. 'That's very kind. Thanks.'

'What's it all about? Is it the mushrooms?' asked Mrs Wilson.

'Mushrooms?' The policeman looked confused. 'What mushrooms?'

Mrs Wilson's face turned crimson. 'Oh nothing... It's cold isn't it?'

A van with 'Crystal Doors and Windows' written on the side pulled up. Two men got out and advanced towards the steps. 'We've come to fix the door,' announced the older looking one.

'I'll be off them,' mumbled Mrs Wilson. 'Just leave the mug by my back door.'

It was lunchtime and the workmen were still repairing the door when Rhian came home. Mrs Wilson went out to meet her. 'You poor dear. Come in and have a warm.' She led Rhian into the kitchen and told her to sit down while she made a drink. 'Where's Gary?'

'He's still at the police station,' replied Rhian quietly. 'He'll be home soon.'

'What did the police want?'

'It's silly really.' Rhian began to smile. 'They said we was dealin' in stolen property and we wosn't.'

Mrs Wilson was no wiser. 'What property?'

'Stamps.'

'Stamps?'

'Yeah. It's going really well only Gary upset a customer. Sold him a one pound brown lilac for five thousand pounds. The man said it was a fake but Gary wouldn't give him his money back. Gary said it was worth thousands more, that he'd got a bargain. The man told the police we was thievin crooks; that we'd stole the stamps.'

'Oh! I thought it was drugs you were selling. The Flying mushrooms. I saw you take the mycelium back to the flat.'

'What?' Rhian placed her elbow on the table and rested her chin in her hand. 'The my silly um died. I threw it out.' Rhian rubbed her eyes and sat up. 'Mrs Wilson, I said I was going to be an entrepreneur. Well Gary and me have. Gary buys old stamp collections, mostly from house clearance, sorts them looking for valuable stamps which we sell. I've built a website and everything.'

'Oh,' said Mrs Wilson.

It was then that Rhian noticed a suitcase by the back door. 'You going somewhere Mrs Wilson?'

Mrs Wilson smiled. 'Yes I am, on holiday to see my son and his family in Japan and on the way I'm stopping in California to spend time with my daughter. I'm so excited. The tickets came yesterday.'

'Lovely,' said Rhian. 'So you aren't going flying mushrooms?' She grinned.

'No,' said Mrs Wilson. 'I'm flying American Airlines.'

They sat looking at the suitcase.

'Mrs Wilson, you got any of that chocolate cake left?'

A Walk in the Woods

4 A Quiet Time In Carmarthenshire

'Rural Carmarthenshire has always been an idyllic, rustic paradise where time moves slowly, dictated by the seasons,' said the website. 'Where autumn follows summer and spring bringing new life to the fields, following the dark months of winter. In the heart of Carmarthenshire, nestling in the Towy Valley beneath the Brecon Beacons, sits the small town of Llangadog. First appearances are of a sleepy village, a place where motorists drive slowly around the dog, sleeping in the road outside the Red Lion - where locals, with time to spare, stop to gossip in the Post Office and the butcher next door knows every customer by name. A quiet tranquil backwater.'

A quiet tranquil backwater. That, if truth be known, was the reason I booked the holiday cottage; to escape and relax, away from my manic life. It was the picture of the dog lounging in the road that clinched it.

The cottage was small and sparsely furnished. The armchair by the fire had been well used. The sort of chair to doze in, with your head resting against the high back. The arm had been patched with a square of faded green material. Dead people's furniture, my father would have called it.

A light drizzle had started to fall. The sky was heavy with dark brooding clouds. I unloaded the car, lit the wood burner and settled in for the afternoon. Ignoring the website warning of limited mobile coverage, I checked my phone for messages.

Nothing. Not one bar and the cottage had no wifi. I was alone, cut adrift from the world. My electronic umbilical cord severed. London, my office, the people I called my friends removed by impenetrable ether. I sat in the chair and closed my eyes.

When I woke the cottage was almost dark, the only light a dim red glow from the fire. I checked my watch, half past seven. My neck ached and a foul taste filled my mouth. I gulped down a glass of water, grabbed my coat and went outside. A gust of icy wind chilled my bones and stung my eyes. A fine spray of rain, like a mist, soaked my face and ran down my neck. I pulled my collar up and walked quickly along the road, past the churchyard filled with, slate headstones and Victorian monuments. Ahead I could see a lamp above an open door, beckoning. I could hear laughter and a murmur of conversation. A woman laughed. The door was open and a ray of brightness flooded out. Beside the door, a granite mounting stone, polished by a thousand rider's boots, shimmered in the wet light. I went in.

The bar of the Red Lion was crowded with drinkers. The place was hot and had the air of a party, of friends letting their hair down, gossiping, telling jokes and flirting.

I pushed my way to the bar. 'A pint of bitter please?'

The barman pointed to the pumps. 'Which one?'

'Which one is local?'I asked.

'Try the Cwrw. That's what I drink,' said a man next to me.

I watched the barman pull the pint. The beer was warm with a distinct hoppy taste, refreshing and comforting. I moved away from the bar and looked for somewhere to sit. All the tables were full except one. In the far corner, beside the window, an old man, reading a newspaper, was sitting at the table. He was wearing a flat cap, a shabby tweed jacket with leather arm patches and a black waistcoat. A farmer, I guessed.

I made my way over to him. 'Do you mind if I sit here?'

'Please yourself,' he replied without looking up from the paper.

It was then that I saw the Collie under the table. I eased a chair over the dog and tried to sit down but there was no space for my legs.

'Get over,' growled the old man and shoved the dog with his foot. He folded the newspaper and slipped it into his jacket pocket. 'You're not from round here?'

'No. I'm from London.'

He removed his cap and scratched his balding head as if carefully considering my answer. 'London.... Yes, yes,' he replied and replaced his cap. 'Holidays is it?'

'Just a couple of days. A short break to get away.'

He nodded. There was an awkward silence. '...I went to Swansea once. Terrible place. All those people.'

I pictured him wandering around a city and smiled. 'Have you ever gone back?'

He slowly shook his head.

'So you prefer things nice and quiet. Llangadog does seem a sleepy place.'

'Nice and quiet! I could tell you a tale or two about Llangadog,' replied the old man and gently tapped the side of his empty glass.

A pint of beer for some stories seemed a fair trade. I went to the bar and returned with two drinks.

The old man took a mouthful. 'We had a murder here in 2003. In this very pub.' He raised his eyebrows.

Now, he had my full attention. 'Really? Where?'

'I was sitting right here, in the bar, when it happened. He was mad, you see, besotted by a younger woman.'

'Who was he?'

'William Davies. He walked into the bar with a shotgun and pointed it at Caroline Evans. She worked here. He was 59 and she was only 27. Pretty girl too. She was six months pregnant and wanted nothing to do with him. He shouted, 'I'll blow your brains out and then shoot myself. We'll go together.' No one moved or said a word. You could hear the clock in the hall ticking as they stared at each other. Then Ben here,' he pointed to the dog, 'growled. He knew something was terribly wrong.'

'Did he shoot her?'

The old man took another sip of his drink. 'The police confiscated his shotgun and charged him with threatening to kill.'

'But you said there was a murder. You said he was going to blow her brains out and then shoot himself.'

'And so I did.' The old man drained his glass, wiped his mouth with the back of his hand and smiled at me. 'It's a wet night. A whiskey to warm my bones.'

I went to the bar again.

'A psychiatrist said Davies was depressed but he was no danger to anyone else. The police dropped the charge of threatening to kill but, in case the psychiatrist was wrong, they kept his gun.'

It wasn't the ending I had expected. 'So no one got killed?' I felt a mixture of relief and ghoulish disappointment.

The old man leaned forward as if to share a secret. His stale breath repelled me but I had to hear.

'He stole a shotgun from a neighbour and came back.' The old man's eyes stared straight into mine. 'He did it. Blew her brains out, just as he said he would, then killed himself.'

I sat back, away from the old man's malodorous face and took a deep breath.

'A barmaid found both bodies when she came to work.'

We sat watching customers at the bar.

A stout man in a Wales rugby shirt was telling a joke. An appreciative group gathered around him. '... then I found someone was accessing my online bank account. I turned detective and found a man from New Zealand I thought was the thief. I confronted the Kiwi but he was slapping his arms and legs and sticking his tongue out. Do you know why?' Rugby shirt paused.... 'He was a haka.'

Groans and laughter greeted the punchline.

The old man rubbed a hole in the condensation on the window. 'It's raining again just like in 1987. I remember the rain didn't stop for weeks.'

He was talking quietly, as if to himself. I leaned forward to catch what he was saying.

'Ben and I were moving some cattle by the river at Glanrhydsaeson when the accident happened. The river was about to burst its bank and flood the fields. Do you see? We had to move the cows to higher ground.'

'What happened?'

The old man turned and faced me. He looked sad. 'The railway bridge collapsed pitching the early train into the river. The driver and three passengers drowned in the Towy that morning. I helped recover the bodies from the water.'

I contemplated what he said. Murder and a suicide in the pub and before that a rail disaster. Not what I'd expected to hear in sleepy Llangadog.

'Are you hungry?' asked the old man. He was smiling. 'They do some excellent bar meals here.' He tapped his empty glass. 'Let's eat.'

I'd had nothing since breakfast and was hungry. It would be rude to sit and eat without inviting the old man to join me and, to be honest, I was enjoying his company. I fetched a menu and more drinks from the bar while he went to the toilet. Ben didn't stir from his place under the table.

'It isn't all death and destruction,' said the old man as he returned. 'Did I tell you I once had a dairy farm of my own?'

I watched him cut a piece of steak and sneak it under the table to his dog. 'No. You said you used to move cows.'

'Before then, I farmed at Gwynfe. Had 36 milking cows. The tanker used to collect the milk every morning and bring it down to The Creamery here in Llangadog. Then, they introduced milk quotas and we knew we had to do something.'

'Milk quotas, when was this?'

'1984. The Minister of Agriculture, Mr Jopling, himself came to explain.' He stabbed to air in front of me with a finger. 'It was our chance to show him a thing or two. Two thousand of us showed up on our tractors. We blocked all the roads trapping the minister for hours and released hundreds of gallons of milk in protest. It was a grand day but I knew the end of milk farming was coming. It was time for Ben and me to do something else.' He shoved a mushroom into his mouth and chewed as he spoke. 'I was right. They closed The Creamery in 2005.'

Did the old man just say it was time to do something else in 1984? I did a quick mental sum.

That was thirty-two years ago. He would have been alive then, but the dog? It must have been a different dog or was the Cwrw affecting my hearing and arithmetic? But then, did it really matter? I felt relaxed. So what if the old man got his dates wrong. He was entertaining and, for the first time in weeks, I felt relaxed and a bit drunk. My break in the country was doing some good.

The barman came over and cleared our plates away.

'Gangsters,' said the old man, 'You have them in London don't you? Krays, Richardsons. I've read about them in the papers.'

'The Krays are dead but we do still have gangs in London,' I replied.

'Ben can smell them, you know; gangsters, he can smell them.'

I looked down at the dog asleep at my feet. 'You have gangsters here?'

The old man nodded. 'The first one was called Malcolm Heaysman, he turned up in 1971 and bought Godrewaun Cottage in the village. Ben didn't like him. He would snarl every time he saw the man and....'

'Just a minute. How old is your dog?'

'I don't really know.' He shrugged. 'I didn't have him as a puppy. As I was saying, he didn't like the man. We were in the lane one morning when a car pulled up. There were two men inside, strangers I'd never seen before. Ben went up to the car and then did something odd, something he'd never done before; he came and sat behind me, almost cowering. They asked if a single Englishman, an old friend of theirs, had recently moved into the village. Oh yes, I said and told them about the man doing up Godrewaun Cottage. They drove off. That's the last I saw of them.'

'What happened?'

'Heaysman was beaten to death by the two men who parked their car and walked across the fields to his house. The police said he was a gangster from Islington, killed to settle an old score.'

I got up and made my way through the hall to the toilet. The Cwrw was stronger than I'd expected. The hall clock chimed the half hour as I returned. Was it really only eight thirty? I wasn't sure. We'd eaten a meal and I thought I'd been listening to the old man for hours. How many drinks had we consumed? Five, six, more; again I wasn't sure. How old was Ben? I no longer cared. It didn't matter. Nothing mattered.

Something had changed in the bar. It took me a moment to understand what exactly. The air was thick with cigarette smoke and the old man in the corner was smoking a pipe. I watched him tamp down the tobacco and strike a match.

He dropped the match into an ashtray on the table. 'Did I tell you about the fire?'

'No. What fire?'

The old man leaned back and blew a smoke ring in the air. 'It was in 1953 or was it 52? I'm not sure now. Anyway, my neighbours, at Glanrhyd Meilock, Mr and Mrs Williams and their children were in bed when a fire started in the kitchen.' The smoke ring had fallen and was settling on the table. He waved it away. 'They escaped down the stairs and out the front door. Mrs Williams told me there so much smoke they had to go down the stairs, backwards, on their bellies. Then she remembered her mother.'

'Her mother. Whose mother?'

The old man raised an eyebrow. 'I just told you, her mother. Mrs Williams' mother, the blind 80 year-old invalid, was asleep in a downstairs room, behind the kitchen. Mrs Williams went back into the house. Her husband tried to stop her. You see, the house was in flames. She told me the fire had spread across much of the kitchen. She crawled across the floor and dragged her mother out. Both women survived but Mrs Williams remained in hospital for some time with serious burns to her back. I used to visit her every week. Of course, I didn't take Ben. Dogs aren't allowed in hospitals.' The old man puffed his pipe, coughed, cleared his throat and sniffed loudly. 'The farmhouse was completely destroyed. We had to do something. I started a collection.' He sat up and pointed to his chest. 'People were very kind. The village collected enough money to completely rebuild the house within a year, imagine that, and Mrs Williams was awarded the British Empire Medal for her bravery.'

Thinking of Mrs Williams crawling across a smoke-filled kitchen, I peered through the smoky gloom of the bar and noticed, the man wearing the red rugby shirt had left. There was something else, all the women who had been there, earlier in the evening, were gone. The room was darker and for some reason, I could not fathom, the landlord had turned off the beer pump's neon signs. I turned back. A youth, I hadn't seen before, was refilling my beer from a large metal jug. 'Thanks,' I said and picked the glass up by its handle.

'Ben did his bit in the war,' said the old man.

I started to laugh. The old man was a fool to be humoured. 'Ben. Which war was that? The Boer War.' I sniggered. 'Was he in the army or the navy?'

'No.' The old man looked offended. 'We were on the mountain. Ben was barking. He'd found a dead man in a gully.'

I stopped smiling. 'A body, who was he?'

'There was three pounds ten shillings in his wallet which I was very glad of and an identity card.'

'You took his money? You stole from a dead man?'

'He wasn't going to spend it, was he? The old man shrugged. 'His name was Sergeant Jones. He'd baled out of a damaged Lancaster bomber. We found the parachute where he came down. The poor sod crawled three miles with a broken leg before dying.'

I'd heard enough. The old man with bad breath was a thief, a liar and a sponger. I'd been buying him drinks all evening. It was time to get back to the cottage. What was the time? I held up my arm to look at my watch. It wasn't there. 'Have you stalen my witch?' I tried again, speaking more slowly. 'Have you stolen my watch?'

The old man was lighting his pipe from a candle on the table. He shook his head.

'What's the candle for? Has the power gone off?'

'Stalen witches you say, power gone off. What do you mean?'

I wanted to explain but the words would not come. I took a mouthful of ale from the tankard in front of me.

'I used to drink with William Powell,' said the old man. 'He wasn't a friend but he had a few bob and was always willing to buy a round for anyone who would listen to his bragging.'

I concentrated on watching the old man's mouth. 'What sort of stories?'

'He lived at Glanaraeth Mansion. One night, when he'd had a good drink, he told me about his trial for killing a servant girl. He was accused of pushing her out of an upstairs window. The jury found him not guilty and he told me why.'

Tired as I was, I wanted to know more. 'Go on.'

'Said he tried to seduce her. He liked the ladies, you see, but she refused to submit. He knew the jury would convict so he bribed them and walked from the courtroom a free man.'

My eyelids were closed when something knocked against my leg. Ben jumped up and growled. A man was spreading sawdust across the bare floorboards with a broom.

'Lay down,' ordered the old man. 'There was a witness, a servant boy who mysteriously vanished.' He covered his mouth with the back of his hand to hide the words. 'Some say Powell killed him and chopped up the body.'

'What happened to him?'

'The boy? Nobody knows.'

No, I mean Powell. What happened to him?'

The old man grinned. 'He built a house next door to this pub and used it to entertain different women. When Bill Williams, he was a draper from Llandovery, discovered his wife had been to Powell's house he was mad with anger but he wasn't the only one wanting revenge on Powell. A gang of them went to Powell's mansion and murdered him.'

'Sounds like he deserved it,' I said sleepily.

'The stupid men left footprints in the snow and were soon caught, all except Williams. He escaped to France.'

I collected my wits and asked the question that I knew he couldn't answer. 'When was this man you used to drink with murdered?'

'What do you mean? You must have read about the murder. It was in all the papers. It was last January.'

'January, yes, no, I mean what year. Tell me the year.'

The old man looked at me as if I was an idiot. 'This year of course 1768. When did you think?'

I stood up and tried to focus. 'You're a liar. That was two hundred and fifty years ago.'

The old man drew the newspaper from his jacket pocket. 'So I lie do I?' He handed the news sheet to me. 'Here at the top.'

I sat down and read the headline. 'Two hanged for Powell Murder, other assassins turn king's evidence to cheat gallows.'

'What's the date?' demanded the old man. 'Tell me the date on the paper.'

It was in small print in the corner of the page. '11th day of September 1768.'

I woke and sat up in the chair. A ray of sunshine illuminated the cottage. I felt awful. The beer monster was taking its revenge for my heavy night. As the details of the evening slowly emerged I realised how ridiculous it all was. I must have been very drunk. How did I get back from the Red Lion? I didn't remember that part of the evening but the old man; I couldn't get him out of my mind. Who was he and where did he get all the ridiculous stories from?

I splashed some water on my face and cleaned my teeth. It was nearly mid day, the pub should be open by now. I walked back through Llangadog, past the church, and on, along Church Street to the Red Lion. A sheepdog was asleep in the road.

'Ben,' I called. 'Here boy.'

The dog stood up, eyed me with distain and trotted away.

I tried the door of the Red Lion. It was locked. A man emerged from the post office opposite.

'What time does the pub open?' I asked.

'It doesn't,' he replied. 'The place has been closed for months.'

I looked through the window. The table where I sat with the old man was in the corner but it was covered in rubbish, discarded cans of pop, sandwich wrappers and an old newspaper. I tried to read the date on the paper but the print was faded. I stepped back across the road and saw a 'For Sale' board fixed from an upstairs window. I began to walk back, towards the cottage and had only taken a few steps when a dog barked behind me. The collie had returned to the Red Lion and was sitting in the road. I'm not sure if the dog's bark was telling me to but I looked up and there, above the doorway, was William Powell's name carved in a slate panel. I was standing outside the house he built before he was murdered.

A Walk in the Woods

5 A Class Transaction

'Fetch Harris',' ordered the Duke of Gwent. He and his son, Viscount William Dunwood were dining at the duke's London club.

The steward, aware of the duke's quick temper, hurried away. He returned moments later with a small book. 'Here you are my Lord, Harris'.'

'Give it to him.' The duke pointed to his son.

Viscount Dunwood took the book. 'Harris' List of Covent Garden Ladies of Pleasure 1816 - First edition published 1773.' He frowned. 'Why are you showing me this?'

The duke reached across the table and plucked the book from his son's hand. 'Because it's time you became a man of the world.'

'I don't understand.'

'Damn it, sir. Must I explain everything?' He flicked through the pages. 'Ah! Capital. Ridden by Harris himself. She'll do nicely.'

Viscount Dunwood sipped his port and waited. The evening had taken an unwelcome turn.

The duke cleared his throat and read an entry, 'Miss Fisher is lusty, has dark hair and good teeth but will not yield to an embrace for less than three guineas which, in the author's opinion, is value for money.' He grunted derisively. 'You look a little red around the gills, sir. Pour yourself another glass. It'll put lead in yer' pencil.'

The Duke of Gwent's carriage was summoned and, after a short ride, a liveried gorilla of a footman showed the two men into the parlour of a fashionable house. A large fire burned in the hearth. Candle light from the chandelier reflected from the gilt furniture. Red and gold drapes cloaked the walls and windows, holding back the cold night air.

A stocky woman, her pock-marked face concealed by rouge, was standing with her back to the fire.

'Madame Josephine, it's good to see you again,' said the duke.

'My Lord Gwent. You are most welcome' She surveyed the viscount. 'And who is this?'

'My son, William Dunwood. I bring him to you to complete his education.' He turned to his son. 'The madame runs one of the finest houses in London... Tell me Madame, Miss Fisher would she serve our purpose?'

Madame Josephine handed the duke a glass of brandy and studied Viscount Dunwood. 'She's a similar age and clean. An excellent choice...'

'Father I...'

'Damn your impertinence, sir. The madame is talking.'

'I'll make the arrangements,' said the madame. She moved to the fireplace and pulled a bell cord.

A maid entered the room and curtsied.

'Tell Miss Fisher she has a gentleman visitor and tell Bruno to attend me in five minutes.'

'Father, I really don't...'

'One moment,' said the madame. The maid stopped by the door.

'My Lord, do you desire some entertainment this evening. Marie is available.'

'Not tonight madame.'

Madame Josephine nodded. 'Go,' she said and waved the maid away.

The footman Bruno entered the room and stood waiting for his instruction.

'Take the viscount up to Miss Fisher.'

He nodded. 'This way, sir.'

Viscount William hesitated.

'Well. go on,' snapped the duke. 'What are you waiting for?'

Bruno showed the viscount out and shut the door quietly behind them.

'He's very nervous,' said the madame.

The duke sat down, drained his glass and held it out for a refill. 'He's a pup, a mummy's boy. Makes me sick.'

The viscount followed the footman, across the hall and up the stairs to the first landing. The maid, her arms laden with bedding, smiled nervously and curtsied as they passed.

Bruno pointed to the next staircase and on they went. The second floor was less ornate. The bedroom doors smaller and closer together. Here, Bruno went ahead, up a narrow staircase leading to the attic rooms.

He stopped at a door, knocked and without waiting for a reply opened the door. He stood back and motioned for the viscount to enter.

The room, dimly lit by just two candles, was austere; a stark contrast to the room three floor below. Brown paint magnified the gloom. The sloping ceiling disorientated the viscount. He flinched as the door closed behind him.

As his eyes adjusted to the dark he saw a girl sat on the bed. 'Are you Miss Fisher?'

'Yes,' replied the girl. She spoke quietly, unsure of herself. 'I'm Nellie.' She didn't move as he approached.

He sat down beside her and they stayed, heads down, without speaking, a tacit understanding of what would follow.

The viscount, nervous and clumsy, performed quickly. Nellie guided him then shut her eyes and thought of John. She always imagined it was John to escape the stale breath on her face, the feel of strange men violating her body, to dull the shame.

Then with one last shudder it was over.

The viscount mumbled incoherently, an apology perhaps and withdrew leaving her alone in the room.

'Well, sir?' said the duke as his son returned to the parlour. 'Is it done?'

Viscount Dunwood grinned sheepishly as his father counted three gold coins into Madame Josephine's hand.

Upstairs, in her attic garret, Nellie turned over and wept silent tears into her pillow. 'Oh John,' she whispered. 'Why?' Every night she prayed for his return but he never did. Gunner Fisher lay buried deep in the mud at Waterloo.

There was a tiny whimper. Nellie Fisher got up, drew back the curtain and held her baby to her breast.

Nellie had returned the child to its crib and dried her eyes when there was a gentle tap on the door.

'Madame says you have another gentleman visitor,' said the maid and scurried away.

A Walk in the Woods

6 The Decoration.

'Did you remember to bring it?' asks Sarah. I check again to make sure it's still there. The silver brooch in my pocket feels warm in my hand. A light drizzle is falling as we wait on the platform. Water drips from a broken gutter on the front of the passenger shelter. Sarah is humming quietly to herself, a cheerful nameless tune. She often hums when she's happy. We stand reading the notice-board. Apart from Sarah and myself the little platform, that is Llangadog station, is deserted. We watch as the train slowly approaches along the single track. I call it a train but really it's just one old, tired, carriage. Behind us a claxon sounds as the level crossing closes. I look at my watch. The train's early.

The guard opens a door and steps on to the platform. He's smiling. 'Bore da, good morning.'

We answer and climb aboard. I know Sarah prefers to travel looking forward and choose seats facing a table. There are three other passengers on the train, a man in his sixties, balding and overweight, a younger woman reading a book and, at the far end of the carriage, a tall thin man dressed as if he's about to climb Everest.

'Did you lock the car?' asks Sarah. She knows I forget to lock doors. Last year we were five miles from home when she asked and I couldn't remember. She made me turn around and drive back to find the front door wide open.

'Yes,' I reply, more sharply than I intend. 'You watched me lock it and you tried the handle.'

The carriage is hot and stuffy. I unzip my jacket and squeeze into the seat.

The diesel engine rumbles and we start to move.

'Tickets please?' The guard inspects our bus passes.

It was Sarah who discovered we could use the bus passes and travel for free on the train.

'Shrewsbury, for the day?' asks the guard.

'Yes,' says Sarah. We go past cars queuing at the crossing. The train gathers speed, 'Clickety-clack, clickety-clack.'

It stops raining. A glimpse of blue, enough to patch a sailor's trousers, appears. The sun is, probing, searching for a gap, looking for a way through the clouds.

We're in the country now, rattling past lush green fields, cows and sheep. There's a different sound, a hollow rumble, as the train crosses the Towy. The water level in the river is high close to breaking its banks, of flooding the meadows and fields.

'Llanwrda,' shouts the guard. The train slows and stops.

School children get on, filling the carriage with noise; an excited babble of conversation and laughter. The balding man pulls a face and hides behind his newspaper.

We are past Llandovery. The carriage is quiet now the children have gone, an adult world of polite personal space, reading and day dreaming. The tall thin man summons the guard and points to his phone. 'The wi-fi isn't working.' He looks cross.

'It's broken,' says the guard and shrugs.

Sarah pours coffee from a flask. We sip the hot liquid as the train trundles across Cynghordy Viaduct.

The train continues on along the single track. Branches brush against the windows spilling dappled sunlight into the carriage.

The train is slower now. Outside all is dark. The noise of the engine is deafening. I can taste burnt diesel fumes. We are in a tunnel climbing towards the Sugar Loaf. Light floods the carriage as we emerge from the gloom.

'The Heart of Wales,' Says Sarah.

We admire the view. Miles of verdant farmland, woods and heath lay before us - a colossal tapestry of shapes and colours. A red kite is circling effortlessly above. I watch a farmer, on a quad bike, drive sheep in the distance.

The train stops at Llanwrtyd. 'We'll be here about ten minutes,' announces the guard, 'waiting for the train from Shrewsbury. You can get out and stretch your legs. Don't worry we won't go without you.'

'Come on,' says Sarah. 'And don't forget your stick.'

We explore the station. There's a smell of fresh paint. Women, planting flowers in a raised bed, are laughing at something. The beds are a riot of red geraniums, blue larkspur and yellow flowers whose name I do not know. A southbound train appears and stops alongside our carriage. Our driver and guard cross the track. This is as far as they come.

'We'd better get back,' says Sarah.

A woman hurries along the platform. With her are three children. She follows us onto the train, scans the carriage and comes towards us. 'Do you mind?' she says and points. 'The table, we want to play cards.' She expects us to move?

'Yes we do mind,' says Sarah and looks at me. 'Some people, really.'

The woman glares and moves to some seats behind us. As she goes by she knocks my walking stick over.

'Bloody thing,' she mutters as she picks it up.

'Tickets? Have your tickets ready,' shouts the guard. It's a different man. He moves quickly through the carriage, checking we've all paid, hoping to catch a dodger, efficient; a jobs-worth.

We are in Knighton, 'Tref-y-Clawdd', the town on the Dyke. Our train crosses the border. There are no border guards, no passport checks. Offa's kingdom lies ahead. The Pillar of Eliseg, with the stonemason's typo, explains all. Welsh mountains give way to the farmlands of England.

'Can we start with the castle? It isn't far. I should be able to walk if we go slowly,' I say as we leave Shrewsbury station.

'Then we'll have lunch,' says Sarah. She knows the regimental museum is there. She knows I want to see the medal.

The curator, an old man dressed in sports jacket and grey trousers is wearing a regimental tie. The immaculate knot, the fresh creases in his trousers

70

and his upright bearing says it all; he was an officer. He leads us through exhibits with a steady commentary. He speaks confidently, with pride choosing his words with care. 'Princess Margaret came here once. I showed her around.' He pauses in the great hall to point out the Mess Silver, fabulous cups and plates in a glass display case. 'She asked me for a fag. Not what you might expect a princess to say.'

I imagine Margaret puffing a Woodbine behind the silver display.

He shows us Grand Admiral Doenitz's baton captured by the regiment when it arrested him.

We reach the medal cabinets. 'These are from the Great War.' He points at a cabinet in the centre of the room. 'Did any of your family serve?'

'My husband's grandfather,' replies Sarah. 'He was gassed at the second battle of Ypres. We have his medals at home.'

Our guide nods approvingly.

'Where do you keep the Whitewash Brigade Medal?' ask Sarah.

He looks surprised. 'The 1894 Hong Kong Bubonic Plague medals? You know about them?' He leads us to another display.

There's a lithograph print of soldiers carrying corpses from a house. 'Soldiers of the 1st King's Shropshire Light Infantry disinfecting plague houses,' says thc title. The silver medal is also there, a polished disc with a yellow and red ribbon. I can see the figure of death on it, hovering over a Chinaman. Sarah reads the card beside the medal.

'An unofficial medal awarded to six hundred men known as The Whitewash Brigade who risked their lives, collecting the dead for burial and fumigating houses.'

There's a second plague medal, a gold one, in the display.

'They were given to the officers,' explains our guide. 'The sad thing is the men were permitted to keep the medals but wearing them was forbidden.'

'Why?' asks Sarah.

'The medals were paid for by the people of Hong Kong. Because they were unofficial decorations, not awarded by the Crown, the men were not allowed to wear them. Shame really. What they did was incredibly brave.' Our guide shrugs. 'Some got turned into watch fobs. I believe others were made into brooches and given to sweethearts.'

I produce the silver brooch from my pocket. 'It was my great grandfather's. He was in the Shropshires. He gave it to his wife.'

'Are you sure you want to do this?' asks Sarah. I know she means well.

I offer the brooch to our guide. 'I'd like to donate it to the museum if that's possible.'

He takes the brooch and studies it. 'Yes. Yes indeed. I must say, that would be a splendid gesture.'

We are on the train approaching Llandovery. It's dark outside. A noisy crowd of teenagers are on the platform. They fill the carriage. Cans and bottles are being opened and drunk. Ribald chatter echoes around the carriage. It's a party.

'Celebrating in Swansea tonight,' says a girl in an alarmingly short skirt, 'the end of A-levels.' She giggles and takes a swig of cider.

We get off at Llangadog and watch the revellers' train vanish into the night.

'I wonder what time they'll come home,' says Sarah and squeezes my hand.

I smile. 'Long after our bed time I expect,' I say.

I'm tired but it's been a good day.

A Walk in the Woods

7 Tom Wellies takes a Bath

Thomas Jones was a farmer and, like other farmers in the valley, he wore wellington boots. In fact, wellies were the only footwear he possessed. As a baby he was given beautiful bootie wellies. He learnt to walk wearing wellies, went to school in wellies and even got married in wellies. Some say it was the sweaty, rubbery smell of his wellies that drove his wife into the welcoming arms of a sheep shearer from Llandybie.

'There he goes,' the neighbours would say, 'Tom Wellies,' and smile at the joke.

One afternoon Tom was on his quad bike, riding home, after taking water to sheep in a field he rented at the bottom of the hill. Windy Hill, as it was known, was steep and there was a cottage at the top called Bryn Awelon. The owner, Mr Hughes, was by the front door scratching his head.

Tom stopped his bike and switched off the engine. 'You look worried Mr Hughes. Is something the matter?'

'My bath,' said Mr Hughes and pointed at a large cast iron bath in the hall.

An odd place for a bath thought Tom. Why wasn't it in the bathroom where it belonged?

Mr Hughes saw Tom's confused expression. 'I'm trying to get it out, to fit a new bath; one with jets.'

'A jet bath! What sort of jets? Why do you want jets?' asked Tom.

'I don't,' said Mr Hughes quietly. He rolled his eyes and nodded towards the kitchen. 'It's a Jacuzzi bath - she wants it. Silly idea if you ask me.'

Mrs Hughes' head appeared in the kitchen doorway. 'Silly idea is it? I'm not deaf. All the famous people have them these days. Jacuzzis are the height of luxury.'

'Oh,' said Tom but he still didn't understand. 'But, Mr Hughes, why have you put it in the hall?'

'It's stuck. I managed to slide it down the stairs but it's too wide, it won't go through the front door,' explained Mr Hughes. 'It's so heavy I can't move it.'

'I'll help you lift it out,' said Tom and got off his bike.

The two men pushed and pulled but the bath was stuck fast, wedged between the bottom of the stairs and the front door.

'It's no good. It's those big claw feet. I'll get a hammer and smash them off,' said Mr Hughes and went to look for a hammer.

Tom was waiting for him to return when William Bale came walking up the hill. William, a big, mild mannered, fellow with hands the size of dinner plates and a face as red as beetroot, was a casual dresser whose coat had lost its buttons years before. To keep it snug he tied it with a belt of baler twine. He didn't care if everyone called him Billy Baler in fact he quite liked the name.

'Billy, you're just the man we need,' cried Tom. 'Come and help us move this bath.'

Billy Baler surveyed the scene and wondered why there was a bath in the hall of the cottage.

Mr Hughes arrived with a big hammer and was about to give the bath an almighty whack.

'Hang on. I've been thinking,' said Tom. 'If we can get the bath out without breaking it I could put it in my bottom field for the sheep to drink from. Billy here will help us turn it on its side.'

'Well boys. Let's give it a try,' said Mr Hughes.

The three men grunted and groaned and, after a lot of arguing and a few swear words, managed to get the bath on its side and push it through the front door and into the road.

'What do we do with it now?' asked Billy.

'I'll get a trailer. I won't be long,' said Tom. He jumped on his bike and roared off. He returned minutes later with a small sheep trailer behind the quad bike.

'You'll never get it in that. The bath's too long,' snorted Mr Hughes.

'We'll tie it on,' said Billy. Tom lowered the ramp on the back of the trailer and the three men dragged the bath in.

'There! I told you it was too long. The bath is sticking out the back. The ramp won't shut,' said Mr Hughes.

'Tie it to the taps with this,' suggested Billy and undid the baler twine around his middle. Tom fastened the ramp to the taps and got on the bike.

'I'm telling you, it's not safe,' said Mr Hughes. 'Look at the tyrcs. They're flat as pancakes and that string will snap. The bath isn't secure.'

Tom considered Mr Hughes' warning and had an idea. He got off the bike. 'You can drive Billy,' he said. Then he climbed into the bath and sat down. 'I'll hold both sides of the trailer firmly. That should do it.'

Mr Hughes watched the bike, trailer and bath, containing Tom, move slowly down the hill. When it disappeared from view, he shook his head, went inside and shut the door.

'Are you alright, Tom?' called Billy Baler. He could feel the trailer pushing the bike down the hill. 'Hang on tight. I can't stop. I can smell burning. The brakes won't hold.'

'I'm fine,' shouted Tom. 'Keep going. We're nearly at the bottom of the hill.'

Billy was relieved when they reached the bottom without mishap. He turned to follow the lane beside the river and, happy they were safely on the flat, gently accelerated. The bike and trailer picked up speed but the bath, loaded with its own inertia, had other plans. It refused to change direction. There was a crack as the string snapped, a bang as the ramp hit the road and a loud screech as the bath containing a very frightened Tom Wellies slid from the trailer.

Knowing something terrible had happened, but not sure what, Billy stopped and looked back along the lane. He saw the ramp was down, and the gouge mark in the road but where was the bath and, more importantly, where was Tom. 'Where are you,' he shouted.

'I'm here,' came a distant cry.

'Where,' shouted Billy.

'Down here,' yelled Tom.

Something on the river attracted Billy's eye. He looked down and watched Tom float slowly past.

'Save me,' cried Tom.

'Is that Tom Wellies sailing in a bath?' asked a surprised fisherman as the unfortunate sailor cruised past Llangadog Common. Passengers on the afternoon train were stunned to see a man, sitting in a bath, drifting along the River Towy. Traffic stopped on the A40 to watch the spectacle. The alarm was raised and the fire brigade called. They stretched a hose across the river in Llandeilo and waited. A crowd cheered from the bridge as they pulled the bath to the shore and rescued the reluctant mariner.

'What shall we do with the bath?' asked a fireman.

'I don't care. I never want to see the bloody thing ever again,' replied Tom and squelched home in his wellies.

A Walk in the Woods

8 The Mart

Carwyn looked at the turkey in the cage and tried to guess its weight. It was a monster - forty pounds at least. An old woman dressed in a greasy jacket sidled up. Her appearance, lank grey hair, hooked nosed and eyes, black as soot, made Carwyn uncomfortable.

'He's got a lovely temperament,' said the woman. 'I'll be sad to see him go.' Her voice, the voice of a fifty a day smoker, rasped like gravel.

'Why are you selling him?' asked Jean.

The question alarmed Carwyn. Was she actually considering buying this beast of a bird?

'I have to. They're moving me to sheltered accommodation. No pets allowed.' She coughed, a long hacking wheeze of intake followed. 'Not even a friendly bird like Thomas.' The old woman wiped a tear from her eye.

Thomas tilted his head and looked wistfully through the bars. Carwyn's wife looked wistfully at the bird.

'No,' said Carwyn. 'Definitely not. We came to buy chickens not a Frankenstein turkey. How would we get it home? Seat belted on the back seat, waving a regal wing at passing cars? No!'

The woman shrugged, coughed again and wandered off.

'Your first mart is it?' A little man wearing brown dealer boots was standing behind Carwyn and Jean. He lifted his cap and wiped his forehead with a dirty handkerchief. 'You were lucky.'

'How do you know it's out first time at the mart?' asked Jean.

'Shiny new green wellies,' said the man and pointed at their matching wellingtons. Heulwen always makes a bee-line for newbies wearing wellies that are too shiny.'

'You said we were lucky,' said Jean.

He tapped the cage with his foot. 'This old bird should have been cooked years ago.'

Thomas turned to face the old man and tried to peck his foot.

'He's a nasty old bugger and tough as old boots. If you get my meaning.' He sniffed hard and cleared his throat. 'Not worth buying? Not if you've got any sense.' He pointed to the old woman who was lighting a cigarette at the far end of the poultry shed.

She threw a match away and did a little dance.

'That's Heulwen. She's here every mart. Always up to something. She's a menace. Would have taken your money and there's something else. This old bird.' He kicked the cage again. Thomas pecked at him. 'It's not hers to sell, by damn. She's bonkers, should be in a loony bin.'

Carwyn and Jean left the man in the flat cap, in the poultry shed and moved outside. The auction had started in the main field. A crowd gathered following the auctioneer as he moved from lot to lot. The bidding was fast and difficult to follow. Piles of timber, plastic window frames, rusty tools, an old toilet and other assorted junk went - knocked down and sold with breathtaking speed.

It had rained hard during the night and the field was a sea of puddles and slippery mud.

'Not so shiny now,' said Jean pointing at their boots.

Carwyn stopped to look at a trailer. 'She's a beauty. All aluminium body, new tyres. Would be very useful. I think I'll buy it.'

'What, to take Thomas home on?' said Jean.

Carwyn scowled at her.

'Give me the bidding card,' said Jean. 'I'm going back in the poultry shed. The bird auction starts at ten. I won't be long.'

'Remember what we agreed. Six hens.' Carwyn handed her the bidding card. 'And if that old woman is back, don't go buying Thomas the Turkey.'

Jean screwed up her nose and vanished into the crowd.

The auctioneer was moving closer. A tall man wearing a long riding coat, standing beside Carwyn examined an ancient cast iron bath. He turned the taps on and off, knocked the side of the tub with his stick and listened. He walked around the bath and bent down as if to inspect the underneath. Then he stood and tried to lift one side of the bath. It didn't move.

'Do you want a hand?' said Carwyn.

'Would you?' said the tall man. 'I want to tip it on its side to look at the drain.'

Carwyn went over and they both tried to lift the bath. Their feet slid in the mud as they strained. It didn't budge. It was as if the bath had been concreted into the ground. A third man joined them and then a fourth. Eventually there was a line of helpers all trying, without success, to lift the bath.

'I think it's the feet. They must be jammed in the mud. Let's try the other side,' said the tall man.

The men all carefully waddled to the other side and, on the count of three, heaved.

'It's moving,' yelled an onlooker.

There was a loud sucking noise. The bath came free, released from the iron grip of the mud. It popped out of the ground with more force than anyone expected. Carwyn let go of the bath and tried to remain upright but the man next to him lost his balance. He grabbed Carwyn's arm, slid and down they went, face first, into the mud. Carwyn used the bath to pull himself up. A boot came off and his sock covered foot slithered away. Down he went again, this time on his bottom where he remained mud-lark like surrounded by a growing crowd of spectators.

The auctioneer arrived and looked down at Carwyn. 'Are you all right?' Then, having made his polite enquiry he went on, 'Lot eighty-seven, cast iron bath with brass fittings. Who will start me at twenty pounds?...'

Carwyn tipped water from his boot pulled it on and crept away.

'Good God. What happened to you?' asked Jean. 'Have you been playing mud pies?'

'I slid over lifting a bath.' Carwyn peeled his jacket off, rolled it in a conspicuous bundle and tried to look unconcerned.

84

Jean looked at Carwyn with her, you're an idiot look. 'You need a bath. Come on.'

Carwyn followed her to the auctioneer's office walking slowly, legs apart, John Wayne like, with stiffening trousers.

People backed away as he went in. A fan heater on the ceiling started to dry Carwyn's hair congealing the slime on his head.

The girl behind the counter looked up. 'Bidding number?' she said and sniggered.

Jean showed her the number. They waited for the invoice to be printed.

'Not all the auctioneer's notes have got to the office yet. You'll have to wait. They won't be long,' said the girl fighting to conceal her amusement.

Minutes passed. Carwyn picked dried mud from my eyebrow. People queuing behind then mumbled impatiently. The office girl doodled with a biro, drawing a line of matchstick men across her blotter. She picked up a brown pencil and added trousers and a shirt to one. Jean rolled her eyes. The printer made a noise and spewed out their bill.

'Two hundred and sixty-four pounds and twenty-six pence,' said the girl.

'What! For six bloody hens.' Carwyn snatched the invoice from her.

Jean turned to face the audience behind them. 'Oh dear. I seem to have a rubber arm. It just wouldn't stay down,' she declared in a stage whisper.

'A rubber arm! You've bought forty hens, sixteen ducks and a rooster. Don't tell me, he's called Rocky... Where are they all going to live?'

'You can build houses for them,' said Jean cheerfully. 'It won't take long. Did you buy the trailer?'

'No,' snapped Carwyn. 'You had the bidding number, remember? Anyway, I thought you didn't want me to buy it.'

'I just thought it might be handy to get the birds home,' said Jean. 'Still, look on the bright side.'

'The bright side? I'm covered in mud. We've spent a fortune on hens we don't have hen houses for. Jean, you've bought enough ducks to start a wet fowl centre when we haven't got a pond. What bright side?'

Jean just shrugged and smiled sweetly.

Carwyn was ramming poultry into the back of the car when a pickup, driven by the tall man with the stick, cruised slowly across the field and stopped beside him. The man wound down his window. 'Thanks for your help. I got it,' he said and pointed to the iron bath on the aluminium trailer he was towing. As he drove away the pickup began to slip. He gunned the engine spinning the wheels, showering Carwyn with mud. The box Carwyn was holding slipped from his hands, split open and out popped the rooster who, with a jubilant squawk, made good his escape across the field.

'So what is the bright side?' asked Carwyn.

'We didn't buy Thomas,' said Jean and pointed to a young couple struggling to lift a large cage containing a malevolent looking Thomas into the back of a van. The turkey, unhappy with being sold, was having none of it; flapping and squawking. It lunged forward and pecked the woman's hand.

She shrieked, let go of the cage and yelled, 'I told you not to buy the bloody thing.'

'Look, they're wearing shiny new wellies,' sniggered Jean and got into the car.

A Walk in the Woods

9 Phil The Bath

Pensioner Percy Thomas was sitting on a bar stool, in the Drover's Arms, enjoying his usual lunch-time pint. 'A low melting alloy - six letters,' he said looking at Dylan.

'Got any letters?' replied the landlord.

'Starts with an 's' and the third letter's an 'l'.'

Both men scratched their chins; Percy because he always scratched his chin when he was thinking and Dylan, who wasn't very bright, because he wasn't thinking anything in particular but felt it was the right thing to do.

'Silver, that's a metal and it fits. It's got to be silver,' said Percy and pencilled in the answer.

Just then Mr Jones came down the stairs at the back of the bar. Of course, no one calls him Mr Jones. His name's Phillip or, Phil and, because of his occupation, everyone knows him as Phil the Bath.

'Is it fixed?' asked the landlord.

Phil put his toolbox on the floor. 'The thermostat's buggered. I've fitted a new one.' He placed the faulty stat. on the bar. 'The boiler's on now. You'll soon have hot water.'

Dylan pulled a pint of Cwrw and handed it to the plumber. 'On the house.'

'Thanks,' said Phil and moved around to Percy's side of the bar.

'You busy then?' asked Percy.

'Not really,' replied Phil, wiping froth from his lip with the back of his hand and peering at the newspaper Percy was writing in. 'It's not an alloy.'

'What?' said Percy.

'Silver, it's not an alloy.'

'Isn't it?'

'No and the melting point isn't low. Silver melts at 960 degrees Celsius.'

Percy sniffed and started to rub out the word.

Now, as well as being clever, being a plumber, in and out of people's houses, Phil knows everyone's business and loves nothing better than sharing a bit of gossip; the juicier the better.

'So what's new?' asked Percy, hoping for some local tit-bit of news.

'Had an interesting job this morning.' Phil placed his glass on the counter and gave a knowing look.

Dylan and Percy moved closer.

'Got a call from Dai Jenkins, you know, the tall chap that lives in the big house on the common. Said he wanted a new bath fitted. When I got there, it wasn't a new bath at all.'

'What do you mean?' asked Percy.

'Dai's tight as they come. You can't get a rusty nail out of him so I wasn't surprised. He'd bought a bath at the mart; an old iron one. It was sat on a trailer outside his house. He expected me to carry it upstairs and plumb it in for him. I asked him why he'd bought it. 'I'll show you why' he said and took me up to the bathroom. 'That's why." Phil pointed at nothing in particular, sipped his beer and went on with his story. 'There was a big hole in the bottom of the bath.'

'A hole? What sort of hole?' asked Dylan.

'Yeah. It was this big,' said Phil and made a circle the size of a football with his hands.

'Why was there a hole in the bath?' asked Percy.

'That's what I wondered. What happened? I asked. 'Jamie did it' he said 'and the little sod flooded the kitchen."

'Jamie,' said Dylan. 'Who's Jamie?'

'Jamie's his teenage son,' explained Percy. 'He's a nice kid but clumsy. Go on Phil. What happened?'

'It was like this,' said Phil. 'Dai and his wife were in Swansea for the day when Jamie invited Donna to the house.'

'You mean that blond girl with a wonky eye and the big..?' Dylan made a weighing motion with both hands.

'Yes Donna with the...' Phil mimicked Dylan's weighing. 'And Jamie had only one thing on his mind.'

Percy sniggered.

'What?' asked Dylan.

Phil rolled his eyes. 'He had it all planned. He'd closed the curtains in his parent's bedroom and filled the room with candles. Dozens of them.'

'Why light candles? Silly bugger could have left the curtains open,' said Dylan.

Phil grinned and lifted his arm, fist raised, phallic like.

'Oh,' said Dylan.

'Imagine it. He invites Donna upstairs. They kiss on the landing. He opens the door. The bedroom's lit like a fairy grotto. Hundred of twinkling candles. The air full of scent.'

'Bollocks,' said Percy. 'You're making it up.'

'Suit yourself,' said Phil and drained his glass.

'How did the hole get in the bath?' asked Dylan. 'Did he - you know?' he added and pumped his fist.

Phil looked down at his empty glass and shrugged.

'What?' said Dylan staring at the glass.

'Get Phil a pint,' said Percy and put a tenner' on the bar. 'I'll have the same.'

'Thanks... No he didn't,' said Phil. 'It was a candle that stopped him getting his end away.' He leaned forward and raised his eyebrows.

Dylan listened as he refreshed the drinks.

'She was willing enough and they were on the bed when it happened.' Phil reached for the pint Dylan had poured. 'Cheers.' He sniffed. 'Jamie'd put candles on the bedside table and, what with their bouncing about, one fell over. At first neither of them noticed. I expect they were a bit preoccupied. Then a pillow began to smoulder.'

'How d'you' know what happened?' asked Percy.

'It's obvious,' said Phil. 'Listen Percy and I'll tell you... Jamie grabbed the first thing he could and started whacking the pillow. Trouble was, it was the jumper Donna'd just taken it off. Fanned by the jumper, the feather pillow really started to burn. It was Donna who put it in the bathroom.'

'If it was ablaze, how'd she do that?' asked Percy. 'She wouldn't have been able to carry it.'

Phil thought for a moment and came up with a suggestion. 'She used Jamie's slippers like a pair of tongs. That's how the hole got there.'

'What?' said Dylan. 'I don't understand.'

'I get it,' said Percy and grinned like a Cheshire cat.

Dylan scratched his chin.

'She threw the pillow in the bath and left it to burn,' explained Phil.

'Oh,' said Dylan. 'At least she had a bit of common sense.'

Phil shook his head. 'They were sat on the bed wondering what story to tell his parents when black smoke started wafting from the bathroom. You see, the acrylic bath was alight. The bottom melted. The pillow was burning through the molten plastic.' He paused waiting for a reaction.

Percy shrugged.

'What do you think they did?'

'I dunno" said Dylan.

'They turned the taps on,' said Phil triumphantly. 'To put out the fire... That's how the kitchen ceiling came down. And the water ruined the new oak floor Mrs Jenkins was so proud of.'

Percy wiped a tear away. 'Did you fit the iron bath?'

'Dai sent Jamic to get some friends to help carrying the bath up stairs. We got it up the stairs alright,' said Phil. 'But his mates kept sniggering and taking the Mickey out of Jamie. Things like, is

93

it true Jamie do nice girls love a candle? You should have used a wick Jamie. Inflame your passion did she Jamie? So you met your match with Donna. It went on and on. Dai was getting cross.' He paused... 'Things got worse when we got the bath on the landing.'

'Why?' asked Percy.

'Dai lost his temper with all the piss taking and told Jamie's friends to bugger off home. After they'd gone, I discovered the iron bath wouldn't fit in the bathroom. The silly sod hadn't measured it. It was too long. When I told Dai I couldn't fit it, the tight bugger really lost it. He started shouting. Said if I didn't sort it he wouldn't pay me. Said it was my fault.'

'Miserable fool. So where is it now?' asked Percy.

'The bath?' Phil grinned. 'It's in the middle of the landing where I left it. He'll have to climb over it to go to bed tonight. Serves him right.' Phil finished his drink and picked up his tool-bag. 'Low melting alloy - six letters. The answer's solder, Percy. It melts at 180 degrees. Every plumber knows that.'

10 Scrumpy

It began with a wheelbarrow full of apples, ripe juicy and ready to be eaten. 'We'll make cider,' announced Rhodri, 'and then we'll have a scrumpy party.'

None of them were sure how to make cider but it seemed a good idea.

'When do your mum and dad get home?' asked Meirion.

'Tomorrow afternoon,' said Rhodri. 'We've got plenty of time.'

'How do you make cider?' asked Meirion.

'We need a press to squash out the juice. That's what my dad used to do,' said Dylan. But the friends didn't have an apple press. They considered the problem.

'We'll tread the apples like they do in France. I've seen it on the television. That'll do it,' said Rhodri.

Meirion wasn't convinced. 'Yeah but that was grapes. How you goin' to catch the juice?'

Rhodri thought for a moment. 'Buckets.'

'Nah'. Buckets won't work,' scoffed Meirion.

'The dustbin. We could use that,' suggested Dylan.

Meirion shook his head. 'It's rusty and anyway there's a hole in the bottom.'

Rhodri picked up an apple and took a bite. 'The bath.'

'What?' chorused the others.

'We'll put the apples in the bath and tread them. It's obvious. We'll leave the plug in and scoop the

95

juice out, said Rhodri triumphantly. 'Come on. Help me get the wheelbarrow upstairs.'

Getting the wheelbarrow up to the bathroom was harder than they expected. Rhodri went first holding the barrows handles while his friends lifted the barrow from below.

'Ah!' shouted Rhodri. 'It's come off.' He held up a rubber handle.

Meirion tried to take the weight. The heavy barrow pitched sideways and gouged a hole in the wall. Apples cascaded down the stairs.

The friends abandoned the wheelbarrow in the hall, carried the apples up to the bathroom in buckets and tipped them into the bath.

'That's not enough,' said Rhodri. 'There's more in the orchard. They'll only go to waste.'

And so the friends filled the bath with apples and took off their shoes and socks. The three of them stepped gingerly into the bath and, holding each other's shoulders, started to stamp on the apples.

'It's no good. It isn't working,' said Meirion.

'They're too hard. My feet hurt,' said Dylan and let go of Rhodri.

Rhodri, who was still stamping enthusiastically, lost his balance and slid, bottom first, into the bath, scything his friends feet from under them. They landed in the bath with a crash, blasting bits of apple across the bathroom.

'You idiot. You let go,' said Rhodri wiping apple pulp off the bathroom tiles.

Dylan wiped his legs on a towel. 'Don't blame me. It wasn't my fault.'

Rhodri picked an apple pip from between his toes, placed it on the back of his hand and pinged it back into the bath. 'Boots. That's what we need. I know. There's an old pair of leather boots in the shed.'

The boots, they decided, needed sterilising and the best way was to boil them. The only pot the boots would fit in was Rhodri's mum's jam copper and it was soon warming on the kitchen stove.

'I won't be long,' said Dylan and left the others to watch the boiling pan.

Rhodri had removed the boots from the stove and rinsed them in cold water when Dylan returned with his guitar.

The intrepid brewers marched upstairs.

'I'll go first,' said Rhodri and laced up the boots. He climbed into the bath as Dylan settled himself on the toilet.

'Ready?' called Dylan and played a chord.

Rhodri nodded and started to hop up and down.

'It's working,' called Meirion.

They took it in turns to dance, strum and sing through the afternoon and into the evening.

Rhodri climbed out of the bath.'I'm tired. Let's have a cup of tea.'

The following morning the friends returned to the bathroom, armed with buckets, a dustpan, a colander and some glasses.

'You scoop and I'll strain,' said Rhodri and handed the dustpan to Meirion. They strained a dustpan of juice into a bucket and Rhodri poured the cloudy liquid into the glasses.

'Cheers,' said Rhodri and took a sip while the others watched. He swilled the drink around his mouth and screwed his eyes shut. 'Eugh! It doesn't taste like cider.'

Dylan giggled. 'It isn't cider yet we haven't fermented it.'

'What's fermented?' asked Meirion. 'How do we do fermented?'

'My dad puts sugar with the juice and just leaves it.'

'Leaves it. What do you mean leaves it?' asked Rhodri. 'How long for?'

'I dunno,' replied Dylan. 'Until it's fermented. A week maybe longer.'

'That's no good. My Mum and Dad are coming back this afternoon.' Rhodri sat on the toilet. 'So that's it. We don't have time to ferment. The scrumpy party's off.' He looked accusingly at Dylan. 'Why didn't you say so before?'

'You didn't ask,' said Dylan.

The three friends surveyed the apple sodden bathroom.

'Come on,' said Rhodri snatching up the dustpan. 'We've got to clear this mess up.' He started scooping the contents of the bath into a bucket. 'Give me a hand.'

'What's that?' said Dylan and pointed at the dustpan.

'Looks like bits of white paint,' said Meirion and picked a piece up. 'Ahh! It's sharp.' He dropped it and sucked a drop of blood from his finger.

'You wimp. The paint must have fallen from the ceiling while we were dancing. Never mind the colander will catch the bits,' said Rhodri. They went back to work. More white bits appeared. Slowly as the level of juice and pulp went down the source of the white was revealed.

It wasn't from the ceiling. The acid from the apples had eaten into the bath's enamel. Every time Meirion scooped, more was flaking away from the bath.

To their horror, the receding tide of juice was exposing bare metal in the bottom of the bath.

'I think you need a new bath,' said Meirion.

Rhodri bit his lip. 'What am I going to tell my dad? He'll kill me.'

'What about painting it?' suggested Dylan. 'Paint it white and he probably won't even notice.'

'You twat. Course' he'll notice,' snapped Rhodri. 'I'm dead.'

It was Meirion who came up with the solution. 'Paint it a different colour and tell him you did it because white's old fashioned. He can't argue with that.'

Dylan picked up his guitar. 'I've got to go. My mum needs some help with the shopping.'

Rhodri didn't think much of Meirion's idea but what else could he do? He went to the shed and returned with a half empty pot of blue paint and a brush. 'It's all I could find.'

'There. It doesn't look that bad,' said Meirion when they'd finished painting. 'I'll see you tomorrow.'

'Blue! Bloody blue. Whatever possessed you?' shouted Rhodri's dad. 'It looks awful.'

'I think the blue looks nice,' lied his mum. Later that evening, wearing her dressing gown and slippers she hurried across the landing, went into the bathroom, turned on the taps and added her favourite bubbles.

Rhodri and his sullen father were in the lounge when her scream echoed through the house.

'Your mother,' shouted Rhodri's father and ran up the stairs. He burst into the bathroom and there sitting in a bath full of bubbles was a strange form; a blue apparition that vaguely resembled Rhodri's mother.

'He's an idiot,' she shrieked. 'He used emulsion paint. Look at me. I'm covered in it.'

Rhodri was surprised when his mother came downstairs and couldn't help thinking, she looked like a Smurf.

11 A Walk in the Woods

Laughter, late one summer evening, was the beginning. I refilled Alice's glass and listened again. There was a shout, shrieks of female laughter and a man's voice, carried from afar by the still evening air.

'I can't see anyone,' said Alice. 'Who do you think it is?'

'Sounds like quite a party,' I said and grinned.

It was a balmy night so we stayed, outside, watching the stars. A full moon, silver and bright, and the faint red glow of charcoal embers were our only lights. Above us bats circled and swooped, feasting in the darkness. The laughter in the woods grew louder - as if amplified by our silent vigil.

The following morning I walked down the hill to post a letter. Mrs Thomas was in her garden watering geraniums. I stopped to admire the flowers and pass the time of day. I told her about the revellers in the woods and it was then that she told me a strange tale.

'I was spraying black spot on the roses,' she said, 'when three young women wandered into the back garden. 'Excuse me' I told them. This isn't a public footpath. They looked confused. One said 'But the path used to be here'.'

'Who were they?' I asked.

Mrs Thomas put down her watering can. 'They wanted to know the way to Pen Arthur Woods. I told them the forestry track was on the left half a mile along the lane and off they went.'

101

'Hikers, do you think?'

She shook her head. 'I don't think so. They were wearing pinafore dresses and were bare foot. Probably hippies. There was something else that was strange.' She paused. 'They all had wet hair - looked like they'd been swimming.'

'How odd,' I said.

'Do you think it was them we heard last night?' suggested Alice when I repeated Mrs Thomas' story. The laughter returned that night and again the next. 'Let's go walking in the woods tomorrow and see if we can find where the laughter is coming from,' said Alice.

We rose early and walked down to the forestry track. An articulated lorry, stacked high with lumber, was parked with its engine running in the gateway. The driver nodded to us as we passed. The roughly made track led uphill into the wood. To each side towered regimented lines of Scots Pines, forty year old giant conifers, a man made forest of silent sentinels. Beyond the conifers we emerged into a clearing, broken ground littered with twisted branches and tree stumps. Between the stumps, encouraged by the light, new life was sprouting - green grasses, wild flowers and rampant brambles. Fresh cut timber waiting for collection was piled beside the track, its scent sweet almost sickly. We came to a fork and turned left walking downhill. Here the forest was different, more natural, oak, ash and hazel growing haphazardly. Clumps of alder, competing with willow for the sun, filled boggy hollows. The track was smaller now, an overgrown path. We stopped in a sun lit glade and rested on a fallen log.

'Look there,' whispered Alice and pointed to the far side of the glade. A wagtail was feeding on the grass. We watched it pecking and strutting from place to place.

It was late afternoon when we stumbled upon a derelict building, a cottage with empty window frames and doorway - a dismal, soulless ruin. A stream trickled into an overgrown pond nearby. The water looked milky and slimy. We climbed, over a rotting door, into the house. An ash tree had forced its way through the crumbling terracotta floor and spread a canopy where the roof had once been. A rusting kitchen range filled the hearth. A cast iron kettle lay on its side on the tiles.

'Can you feel it?' asked Alice. 'The house is cold. It feels sad.'

'Nonsense,' I said. 'You're cold because you're out of the sun. Come on. It's getting late. We'd better get back.'

That night the wood was silent. It stayed silent for a month and then the laughter returned. I know it was a month because, as before, the moon was full.

'Let's go to Pen Arthur tomorrow night,' said Alice. 'We'll follow the sound and find out what's happening.'

The sun was setting as we entered the wood. Dusk gave way to an impenetrable gloom under the pine trees. The torch I'd brought shone bright showing the way forward along the track. The moon appeared over the horizon as we reached the barren waste of cut trees. The silver rays cast strange ghostly shadows which followed us. Then the laughter started. We walked on and on towards the sound. And yet, even though we moved towards the noise, it seemed no louder.

I stopped. 'I've no idea where we are. Is this a good idea?'

'Shhh!' said Alice. 'I think I heard a man's voice. They're close.'

A strange chill descended, penetrating our bones. A trickle of cold sweat ran down my back.

'We've been here before,' whispered Alice. 'Look.'

I didn't believe her at first and then I saw the chimney. We were at the derelict cottage but it was different. Moonlight lit the front and side while the rest was in deep shadow. A wisp of smoke drifted from the chimney. The smell of a log fire beckoned. Candlelight flickered from the window. A man pushing a wooden wheelbarrow appeared from the shadows behind the house. He stopped at the front door and set down the barrow.

'Stay out of the water,' he called.

'This isn't possible,' I whispered. I felt content, warm and safe, unafraid of the apparition we were spying on. I knew there was no danger, only love and enchantment. 'Who's he talking to?'

'They're there by the pond,' said Alice.

Three girls were standing on the grass. An older woman was sitting on the bank in front of them with her feet in the water. The girls stepped into the water and started to splash about. They held hands and began to dance in a circle. Slowly at first then faster, whirling like Dervishes, shrieking with laughter until, giddy with excitement, they fell down.

The woman screamed, a hideous piercing screech of anguish. The trees shook as her pained cry echoed through the wood. Darkness obliterated the scene as the moon slid behind a curtain of cloud.

I switched on the torch and shone it on the pond. A shaft of tepid light pierced the gloom. Nothing moved on the oily surface. The old woman was gone. I turned the beam towards the house. The ruin was in darkness, broken and deserted. I felt afraid and started to shake. The cold of the night had returned.

The first light of day was pushing the night sky west as we trudged home along the lane.

'What time is it?' asked Alice.

'A quarter past four,' I replied.

A light was on in Mrs Thomas' cottage.

'She's up early,' said Alice.

The old lady appeared in the doorway and waved. 'The kettle's on if you would like some tea.' Her kitchen was small and cosy. Fresh herbs hanging from the ceiling filled the room with scent. A cat asleep by the Aga ignored us as we shuffled in and sat down. Mrs Thomas poured tea into brown beakers and sat down opposite us. She pushed a plate of Welsh Cakes across the table. 'I made them yesterday. Go on.' She took a bite of one and sipped her tea. 'You went into Pen Arthur Wood to find them didn't you? The girls.'

'They were at a house,' said Alice, 'and there was a man.'

Mrs Thomas nodded. 'That would be Mr Price... I used to play in the woods when I was a little girl. My mother told me never to go near there. She said a witch lived in the house who would do terrible things to me. It was nonsense of course. I went once. I was curious. I'd never seen a witch. I crept through the wood to the house to spy on her but she wasn't there. It was empty and falling down. Nobody lived there. Later, after my mother passed away I learned why the house was abandoned. Years ago a family, the Prices, lived there. Mr Price was a forester and his wife a herbalist. People would come from miles around to buy her potions.'

'I don't understand,' I said.

'Mr Price.' Mrs Thomas took another cake. 'They say he was driving his daughters through Llangadog in a cart and were crossing the bridge over the River Towy when the pony went berserk. It smashed the cart against the parapet, tipping it into the river and bolted. They were all drowned.'

'How awful,' said Alice. 'What happened to Mrs Price?'

'She was a broken woman, alone; her whole family gone. At first, neighbours tried to help, to console her, but she grew bitter and spiteful. People stopped visiting. People called her mad. Some said she was a witch, casting evil spells, trying to conjure her husband and children back to life. One day she vanished. They found her body in the pond. The house has been deserted ever since.' Mrs Thomas smiled at us and pushed the plate across the table. 'Go on, have another Welsh cake.'

A Walk in the Woods

12 The Reckoning

'Due to me this day £4. 7s and...'

Ink falls from the nib onto the page. It runs, like a tiny black stream, across the words. I return the pen to the inkwell and blot the mess. The kitchen door opens. Water drips across the tiles. A bucket scrapes the floor. Jane is humming as she places it by the fire. She always hums when she works; a busy tune - a rhythm to pace herself. She removes her coat and puts on a clean pinny, tying it at the front. I watch her press a loaf tight against her chest, butter it and cut a wafer thin slice. My mother used to slice bread the same way. Plum jam is in the china bowl she fetches from the cupboard. I close my diary.

It's been a long year. Last winter was so cold the river turned to ice. So cold our sow froze in her pen. I found her stiff and lifeless. Snow blocked the lane until March.

Jane places a cup and saucer on the table. Both are chipped and cracked. Her best cups, for admiring, are on the dresser. She lifts a pot from the hearth and pours. I tip the steaming tea into my saucer and blow to cool the scalding brew. I sip from the saucer, still too hot. I blow again.

The breakfast things are cleared away. Jane takes the bucket and fills the kettle hanging in the chimney. She adds twigs to the red embers. They burst into life, spitting and crackling. Flames dance across the grate. I watch her carve a wedge from the

flitch of bacon curing above the hearth. She dices
the meat and adds it to the stew-pot warming beside
the oven. By tonight the meat will be tender.

Spring came late and I was greatly relieved by its
arrival. The snow gone, the roads passable and, at
last, I had a chance to work, to earn some money.
Mr Davis' barn needed a new roof. He offered me
three pounds to do the work. I borrowed his cart and
old nag to fetch timber from the railway station.
Driving down into the valley I stopped in the river
to let the horse drink, to soak the wheels and tighten
the rims. The station master, in his crisp uniform,
stood and watched me with suspicion as I loaded
the stout oak planks. The rough sawn timber was
heavy, like iron. We left the station at a slow walk.
Climbing from the valley the horse strained in its
traces then stumbled, regained its footing and
stopped. I used the whip but the animal was finished
and refused to go a step further. Three days it took
me to haul the timber to the farm.

Mr Davis is a careful man, some say mean.

'You abused my horse.' He spat on the ground.
'And damaged my cart.'

Two weeks of sweat and all he would pay was
one pound eight shillings; scant reward for my
labour. But, it was money and I was sore in need of
it.

The day he paid me I bought Jane a fine red
shawl for two shillings and four pence. She was
pleased with her present but refused to wear it.
Instead, she carefully folded it in brown paper. 'It's

too new for every day,' she said and packed it in the drawer where she kept her special things.

My diary is open again. I flick back to July, a sad time for us all. We buried our dear boy Jacob that month. Scarlet fever took him from us three days before his fourth birthday. I shudder to remember his screams as the doctor shaved his head and scraped pustules from his scalp. Poor Jacob struggled, as I held him tight, writhing to escape the leeches clinging to his temple.

'They will remove the poison from his blood,' explained the doctor, but the leeches didn't remove the poison. He was a brave little boy til the end. I used some of Mr Davis' oak, off cuts I'd taken, to make his tiny coffin. Jane lined it with a grey blanket to keep his little body warm in the ground.

The snow has started again. Wind is blowing flakes through a crack in the kitchen door. Jane points to the fire. I take my coat from behind the door and fetch wood from the shed. The yard is covered in brown slush.

'Will next year be the same?' I wonder as I stack logs by the fire.

A whimper from the crib. Alice cries. Jane picks her up and holds her to her breast. Alice sucks greedily.

We christened Alice last August one week after we laid Jacob to rest. It was a hot day. Villagers filled the church that Sunday and welcomed Alice into the world but I cried as we passed the little pile of earth covering where Jacob lay.

Jane has changed the baby and she sleeps. There's a knock at the door, loud and insistent. I know who it is; the rent collector, Mr Williams. The door opens. Uninvited, Mr Williams steps into the kitchen chilling the room with cold air. Dirty snow falls from his boots.

'Do you have it?' he demands.

I take the money tin from the dresser, count out ten shillings and hand the coins to him.

'It's not enough. You're six weeks behind. I require another thirty shillings or the bailiffs will be calling,' he growls.

'Sit down Mr Williams,' says Jane. 'The kettle is boiling. I'll make some tea.'

Mr Williams removes his hat and sits awkwardly at the table. I shut the diary and move it away from him. Williams is a brute of a man, a bully, but Jane has his measure. She smiles at him as she pours the tea then busies herself around the kitchen. Has he noticed her face is turned away?

He drinks, tells us he's a reasonable man, that he'll give us an extra week to find the money we owe. He smiles at Jane, lecherous swine, and goes on his way, to the next cottage where the scene will likely be repeated. Jane isn't smiling, now he's gone. I make a note of how much we've paid Mr Williams in my diary.

Frost and foggy mornings warned the year was turning. It was September. The days grew shorter, the nights colder. I worked until dusk each day to lay Mr Hughes' hedges. He owed me £2. 4shillings and promised to pay before Michelmas but the 29th

September passed and he didn't honour the debt. I killed our weaner on the 30th. Jane helped gut the pig and salt the meat. We would not starve this winter. Mrs Jones traded us a sack of flour for a bowl of brawn Jane made from the pig's head. Jane interrupts my thoughts. 'You must find the money for the rent man.'

I promise I'll see farmer Hughes and get what he owes me. It's a faint hope but I can't tell Jane that he has no money for fear of worrying her. The mixing bowl comes out. She removes the cloth covering the risen dough, kneads it once more and sets it on a baking tray to rise again. Satisfied it's ready, she pushes it into the hot oven. The door shuts and latches with a metallic click. As I write my journal, the kitchen fills with the smell of baking bread; warm, comforting, safe. How lucky we are, how lucky I am. God has blessed us this last year but he has also tested us. Did he take little Jacob because I doubted him? I shudder at the idea, the cruelty of such a God.

'You missed two Sundays,' said the vicar after Jacob's funeral. 'God is watching us all. He knows everything.' The vicar is a pompous, pious man. I've never liked him.

October brought great excitement to the village. The Queen was coming. Our Queen, Empress of three quarters of the world would soon be here. We dressed in our Sunday clothes and walked three miles, through the mud, to the railway station. A hawker was selling paper flags for two pence each. We stood on the platform and waited. Jane looked grand in her fine new shawl, her face as rosy as the red wool. She wrapped the shawl around Alice to keep out the cold. Someone started to sing, 'Rule Britannia, Britannia rules the...' Others joined in. 'Britains never, never, never will be slaves...' We were excited and proud. Victoria, our Queen was coming.

A steam whistle echoed along the valley; shrill, discordant.

'The Queen. A train. The Queen's coming,' yelled a youth.

'God save the Queen,' chorused the crowd as the train approached.

The engine passed with a roar, hissing steam, belching soot and black smoke. We strained to glimpse the royal passenger in the carriages as they rattled past. The windows were misted, blinds drawn.

Jane screamed and clutched at her face.

'It's burning,' she shrieked. Something was in her eye, a hot cinder blown from the engine. And then, the train was gone. Her right eye was red and weeping. Walking home, we stopped at the stream and bathed it.

'Did you see her, the Queen?' asked Jane.

That terrible October day when Jane lost her eye is seared in my memory.

I open the diary at today's date, 31st December 1866, dip my pen in the inkwell and complete my annual reckoning.

'Due to me this day   £4. 7s   6d.
I owe   £2. 18s 11d.

Balance in my favour   £1. 8s   7d.

May God watch over us and grant us a good life in the coming year.'

The ink dries slowly on the page. Another year is done.

A Walk in the Woods

13 Edwin's Adventure

Edwin Jones didn't stray far from home. He'd been
to Swansea once and didn't like it; all the people
and the noise. 'Never again,' he'd said on the way
home and that was it. He never again left the
village, that is, until the day of his great adventure.

It began like any other day. Edwin was up early,
sitting in his back garden, enjoying his first cup of
tea of the day. He shaded his eyes from the sunshine
and watched a wren going about its business by the
vegetable patch. The little bird entranced Edwin as
it flitted from stalk to stalk. In fact Edwin was so
occupied he didn't hear the knock on the front door.

'Silly sod,' muttered the postman. 'Probably still
in bed.' He knocked again. Still Edwin didn't come.
'Edwin there's a parcel,' he called but still Edwin
didn't come and this vexed the postman. Edwin had
never had a parcel before and this one was a
peculiar shape. What's more it had come all the way
from Australia. The label said fragile and some of
the string holding the brown paper was loose. The
postman tried to peep inside but it was no good.
Whatever it was, unless Edwin came soon, the
postman would never know.

The disappointed postman waited a few more
minutes, scribbled a note, shoved it through Edwin's
letterbox and returned the parcel to his van.

Edwin was in the hall dusting the photograph of his
dear departed mum and her sister Ethel. 'Hello

117

mum. Hello Aunty Ethel. How's Australia?' he said. Then he noticed a piece of paper on the doormat.

He picked it up and read, 'You were out when I called to deliver a parcel. Was I?' he said. 'Your parcel has been returned to the depot.'

Edwin considered the note. He didn't remember going out and resolved to walk to the post office to find out what it all meant.

The postmaster Mr Price listened to Edwin's enquiry about a parcel being returned. 'It's not here,' he explained.

Edwin persisted and showed Mr Price the note that had been pushed through his letterbox.

'Let me explain,' said Mr Price. 'This isn't the depot. This is the post office.'

Edwin scratched his head. 'Yes, the post office.'

'Your parcel will have gone back to the depot. It says that on the note. You have to go to the sorting office in Llandeilo. That's where your parcel was taken.'

'But you said the depot.'

'Yes. The depot.'

'So why do I have to go to the sorting office?'

Mr Price scratched his head. 'It's the same place.'

'Oh!' Edwin's heart sank. Llandeilo was ten miles away and that meant getting a bus. He remembered the terrible day in Swansea and shuddered. Was it worth it? Was any parcel worth the sacrifice? He'd almost decided not to go when a thought occurred to him. It might be an important parcel even something valuable. Yes - he had to go.

The ten o'clock bus was parked at the bus stop when Edwin arrived. The driver, an unshaven, overweight fellow wearing a dangly gold earring, was reading a newspaper.

'I need to go to Llandeilo,' said Edwin, 'to collect a parcel.'

'That's nice,' said the driver without looking up from his paper.

Edwin waved his free bus pass at the driver, sat down and waited. 'What time are we going?'

'Ten o'clock,' said the driver and went on reading.

The minutes ticked by.

Edwin looked at his watch. 'It's ten past.'

'Not by my watch it isn't,' mumbled the driver. He sniffed and turned a page.

Edwin was wondering if they would ever leave when he heard the rhythmic tap of hob nail boots. He looked up and saw the vicar hurrying along the road.

'Wait for me,' came a plaintiff cry.

The driver looked up, thrust the paper behind his seat, closed the door, and with an enormous engine roar, they were off.

Edwin held on grimly as the bus gathered speed. He waved to the vicar as they passed and was surprised to see the vicar shake his fist in return.

'Why did you do that?' asked Edwin. 'It wasn't very nice.'

'What?' said the driver.

'Leave the vicar behind.'

'I don't like him. That's why.'

119

'You will let me off at Llandeilo?' called Edwin as they raced along the main road.

The driver didn't answer.

'I've got a parcel to collect from the sorting office.'

'I know. You told me. What sort of parcel?'

'I don't know. That's why I'm going to Llandeilo to find out.'

Luckily for Edwin the driver did stop at Llandeilo.

'Thank you,' said Edwin as he got off. He was no sooner on the pavement than the doors were shut and the bus was gone leaving a cloud of dust and fumes.

Edwin found the sorting office and went in. He stood in front of the little counter and waited for someone to come. No one did.

'Hello,' he called.

No one answered.

'Hello,' he called again and again, then he saw the button on the counter. A bell rang somewhere in the bowels of the building. He pressed the button again.

Suddenly a door burst open and a short red faced man appeared behind the counter.

'Hello,' said Edwin.

'Why do you keep yelling hello?'

'I wasn't yelling.'

'Yes you were. I distinctly heard you yell hello three times.'

Edwin couldn't deny he'd yelled hello three times. He handed the postman's note to the red faced man. 'I've come to collect a parcel.'

'It isn't nice, you know, yelling at people.'

'I'm sorry,' said Edwin.

'People are always coming here and yelling hello at me. How would you like it if everyone yelled hello at you?'

'I wouldn't,' said Edwin.

The red faced man examined the note. 'Identification.'

'Pardon.'

'Identification. You have to prove you're Mr Jones.'

Edwin hadn't expected this complication. 'What sort of identification?'

'Something with your picture on. A passport will do.'

'I don't have one.'

'Driving licence?'

'I don't drive.'

'Oh dear.' The red faced man frowned. 'I'll tell you what. Two utility bills in your name. But they must have your address on.'

Edwin shook his head.

'That's it then. No identification, no parcel. It's the rules.' The red faced man handed Edwin's note back. 'Sorry. Come back with some identification with a picture on and I'll give you your parcel.'

Edwin moved towards the door. 'What sort of picture?'

The red faced man rolled his eyes and said very slowly, 'A picture of you.'

'Oh,' said Edwin and took out his bus pass. 'I've got this. It's got my name on it and a picture.'

The red faced man examined it, holding it up comparing the picture with the man in front of him claiming to be Edwin Jones. 'The note.' He held out his hand.

Edwin waited for the red faced man to fetch his parcel.

'It's a funny shape,' said the red faced man as he returned. 'What is it?'

'I've no idea,' said Edwin and went on his way.

He got strange looks from the people at the bus stop. Why, they wondered, was he carrying a giant banana wrapped in brown paper.

A tattooed man standing at the back of the queue stared at Edwin.

'Wot' you got there... a dildo?' he sniggered. 'It's a dildo in' it.'

Edwin blushed at the idea.

'What is it?' asked a spotty youth.

'I've no idea,' replied Edwin.

The bus arrived.

'You got your parcel then,' said the driver with the dangly earring. 'It's a funny shape. What is it?'

'I don't know,' said Edwin.

A little old lady sat down next to Edwin on the bus. 'What's that?' she asked, pointing to the parcel.

'I've no idea,' came Edwin's reply.

'Wot' you mean my tickets not valid,' bellowed the tattooed man.

'It's got yesterday's date on,' announced the driver. 'You'll have to get off.'

The tattooed man grabbed the driver by the neck and lifted him up. 'Yea' An you'll make me will ya'.'

'No,' squeaked the driver.

The little old lady got up. 'Young man. You're being very rude. Put the driver down before you hurt him.'

The tattooed man let go of the driver and shoved the old lady back into her seat. 'Shut yer' face you silly old bat.' Then he looked around the silent bus filled with passengers, all staring at him, and his courage evaporated. He turned and jumped off the bus.

'Someone should teach the lout a lesson,' said the old lady to Edwin.

'Someone should,' he replied awkwardly.

She looked at him expectantly.

Unsure how to teach a lout a lesson but feeling it was his duty Edwin got up and stepped off the bus followed by the rest of the passengers. But what should he do next? The tattooed man was making his escape.

Edwin didn't know why but he lifted his parcel and threw it with all his strength in the general direction of the retreating figure. To his amazement the parcel soared through the air spinning like a top. The parcel hit the tattooed man on the head, sending him sprawling and even more amazingly the parcel came back to Edwin who, despite being utterly confused, caught it.

The passengers applauded and patted Edwin on the back. The little old lady gave Edwin a hug as the police arrived and took the tattooed man away.

Edwin sent a photograph of the newspaper cutting of his award ceremony to his Aunt Ethel in Australia. In the photograph Edwin is proudly holding his famous boomerang and the medal they gave him for being so brave.

14 Pigs on Weed

Emlyn Jenkins was a careful, quiet man, balding, small in stature and content with his lot. A man who took his time to reply, to consider a question before he spoke, to roll every word around his tongue testing it for taste for precision, a habit which caused some to think him slow.

Emlyn never argued with his wife. Beryl took all the decisions. She wore the trousers, a matriarch whose stare could reduce a child to tears, whose very presence could intimidate grown men. Their daughter Carol, a bouncy teenager, who had outgrown her passion for horses and discovered boys, was in her mother's image; big, loud, confident beyond her years and as bossy as her mother. Such was the nature of the Jenkins household; commanded by a dominatrix, her apprentice and Emlyn - always the submissive partner.

The idea of keeping pigs had never occurred to Emlyn. He'd never touched a pig, except the sort you have with apple sauce, but after Beryl's dream, a vision of what might be, it was decided. They would buy a pig.

First Carol's horse, a docile nag called Winnie, went to the mart at Llanybydder. Carol cried as Winnie was auctioned but, as the hammer came down, Beryl gruffly observed, they were crocodile tears more for herself than the horse whose fate, probably as a Frenchman's steak dinner, Carol cared less about than she pretended.

'You never liked Winnie. I hate you,' snapped Carol and stormed off.

'Emlyn, you need to reinforced the paddock fence with a stout bottom rail,' said Beryl as they were driving home. 'I don't want the pig escaping.'

Beryl then told Carol the sixty-five pounds from the sale of Winnie was going towards the pig.

'Not fair. Winnie was mine,' replied Carol and sulked all the way home. She texted William, her latest love, *Not fair. My horse. FFS. It's my money. XXX*

William, encouraged by the kisses, replied immediately, *Yea, right, not fair.* Then, as an afterthought, he sent a second text containing five kisses, an angry face and a horse meme.

The following day Emlyn used salvaged corrugated sheets to build a sty for the newcomer and spent the afternoon nailing an extra rail along the bottom of the paddock fence. Then, he drove their estate car to a farm in Powys while Beryl said in the passenger seat giving directions. Carol, still angry about the money was in the back munching an apple.

'Don't make a mess Carol. You know how your father likes to keep his car clean.'

Carol scowled, pushed the half eaten apple into the seat pocket and sat looking at her phone.

The farmer, a grumpy man, with a permanent lop-sided scowl was expecting them. He led the family across the muddy yard to a barn where a large sow was lying on some straw. 'This is Enid. She's a lovely girl.' A large dewdrop appeared on the tip of the farmer's nose. It bobbed up and down as he breathed threatening to fall. He sniffed and it vanished. 'She'll farrow in six weeks time.'

'On the phone you said four hundred pounds,' said Beryl. 'We'll give you three. Pay the man Emlyn.' Her voice was authoritative as if the deal was struck.

Emlyn carefully counted out three hundred pounds and held the money up.

The dewdrop had reappeared on the farmer's nose. He wiped it on the palm of his hand and proffered it to Beryl. 'Four hundred pounds is what I said. For the sow and don't forget she's pregnant. You're getting the piglets for free. Take it or leave it.' He waited for Beryl to shake on the deal.

Beryl looked at the soggy hand, puffed herself up to her full height and glared at the farmer. 'Three hundred and fifty.'

He glared back, or at least that's what Beryl thought. She didn't know his lop-sided face only had one real eye. The other, the one Beryl was intently staring at, willing him to give way, was made of glass. It was a war of wills Beryl would never win. Time passed...

'You're an 'ard woman. Fair play.' The farmer withdrew his sticky hand and turned away. 'Suit yourself.'

Beryl was beaten. 'Don't stand there with your mouth open Emlyn. Pay the man his four hundred pounds.'

Carol sniggered.

The farmer counted the money and stuffed the notes into his jacket pocket. 'There we are then.' He grunted, put a finger over one nostril, sniffed and strode back to the farmhouse.

'Will you put Enid in the car for us?' called Beryl.

'She's your pig. You load her up,' replied the farmer and went indoors.

'Emlyn, put the pig in the car.'

It was at this point that Emlyn learnt Enid was as obstinate as his wife. Enid had no intention of climbing into the back of an estate car. He coaxed, cajoled and pleaded with the sow. He pushed but it made little difference. Enid was content to walk anywhere other than in the direction of the car. Emlyn trotted after her around the muck heap, through muddy puddles and back into the barn.

'Don't just stand there Carol,' said Beryl. 'Help your father.'

The farmer, watching from the house, smiled to himself as the procession of Enid, followed by Emlyn with Carol bringing up the rear circled the yard.

Then Carol remembered the half eaten apple she'd squashed into the seat pocket. She showed the apple core to Enid and backed towards the car. The pig grunted and followed, enticed by the smell of fruit. Carol slid, bottom first, into the back of the car. Enid followed and landed on the unfortunate girl causing her to drop the apple. Emlyn quickly shut the back door trapping both pig and girl. Carol shrieked, 'She's squashing me,' while Enid, determined and excited by the prospect of a tasty snack, rooted about for the apple.

It took some time for Enid to settle down and for Carol to escape over the back seat. Satisfied that the pig was, at last, secure Emlyn started the engine and set off for home.

Carol texted William. *Have pig in car NGL Stinks*

He replied. *What? A pig? XXX NGL you are beautiful*

Carol smiled. *Aww TY*

William was on a roll. *DEF You coming out tonight?*

What time? replied Carol.

'What's that smell?' asked Beryl. 'Has someone been muck spreading?'

'Oh God! It's gross. I can't breathe. Quick open the windows,' yelled Carol. 'The pig's done an enormous poo. Now she's peeing everywhere.'

'Do something Emlyn,' shouted Beryl. 'It's awful.'

'Emlyn slowed the car, opened his window and continued on with his head half out.'

Carol held her nose and texted. *Gonna die. Pig's shit in boot.*

ROFL came the reply.

ROFL?

Roll On Floor Laughing

She answered. *WYCM*

Wot?

Will You Call Me?

Enid soon settled into her new home. She took up residence in the sty and seemed to enjoy scampering around the paddock looking for things to eat.

Beryl hadn't considered the issue of food for the pig. She was a big picture woman not concerned with petty details. Such things were Emlyn's responsibility. Fortunately he'd already thought of it, and bought two twenty-five kilo bags of sow nuts from a merchant, together with a metal dustbin to store the food in. Metal, he reasoned, was best to keep the food dry and other animal from helping themselves. Emlyn tipped a bucket of feed into Enid's trough and watched as she tucked in enthusiastically. The trough was empty in moments.

'She must be hungry,' thought Emlyn and refilled it. The same thing happened again.

'You've got tin legs Enid,' muttered Emlyn filling the trough for a third time. 'That's half the feed gone.'

The following morning he returned to the paddock and was dismayed at what he saw. A bloated looking Enid was laid in the mud surrounded by mushy looking sow nuts. What was left of the feed was ruined. Near the prostrate pig was an empty dustbin and, beyond the bin, a flattened lid. The pig didn't move while Emlyn salvaged the bin but lay there glassy eyed. He chained the bin to a fencepost, straightened the lid as best he could and went to buy more feed.

Beryl, meanwhile, was busy arranging the next part of her plan while involved a cafe on the High Street in Llandovery or rather premises which had once been a cafe.

Mrs Price had shut the cafe, after winning ten thousand pounds on the lottery and the business had been gathering dust for several months. She was happy to pass it on and agreed a modest rent. 'Are you going to change the name?' she asked handing the keys to Beryl.

'I'm going to call it The Pork Chop,' replied Beryl.

Mrs Price frowned. 'Why?'

Beryl smiled and produced a sheet of paper. 'I haven't printed it yet but here's the new menu.'

Mrs Price took the paper and read aloud. 'Pork sausages, leek and pork sausages, pork and chilli sausages, bacon, smoked bacon, belly of pork, pork scratchings, crispy trotters, liver and bacon, ham salad, brawn, liver pate, faggots, roast pork, gammon and egg... Are they all pork?'

Beryl nodded enthusiastically. 'From our own pigs. It's a great idea don't you think?'

'Oh,' said Mrs Price returning the menu.

As the farmer had predicted, Enid gave birth to a litter; fourteen piglets including a runt. By then Emlyn had cleaned the cafe, painted it, inside and out, and hung a sign above the door. He was standing, with Carol, admiring the sign when a young man wearing tight trousers, a bum freezer jacket and carrying a notebook stopped on the opposite side of the road.

They watched as the young man produced a mobile phone and took several photographs of the cafe.

'Are you from the Carmarthen Journal, here about the advertising?' called Emlyn.

The young man wrote something on his clipboard and crossed the road. 'I'm from the council.' He handed Emlyn a business card.

'Dr. Vincent Rees. Town Planning Officer.'

'What are these letters?' asked Carol.

The young man pointed at the letters after his name. 'BSc (Hons) Bachelor of Science with honours, MSc Master of Science, RTPICTP you probably know that's Royal Town Planning Institute Chartered Town Planner and PhD that's my Doctorate of Philosophy.' I did that one at Aberystwyth University.' Vincent Rees paused to let his important education register. 'My thesis was on the design of superior traffic calming humps.'

Carol flicked her hair, provocatively and smiled at Rees. 'Vincent, that's a nice name.'

Rees blushed. 'I'm also a member of the IHBC but there wasn't room on the card.

'The what?' asked Emlyn.

'The Institute of Historic Building Conservation.'

'Impressive,' said Emlyn and returned the business card.

'What is it?' Rees pointed at the sign.

'That,' said Emlyn earnestly, 'is a pork chop.'

'It looks like a sheet of plywood shaped like Africa.'

'I told him it looked odd,' said Carol.

'I haven't painted it yet.'

'You need planning permission for a pork chop,' said Rees.

'I told him that. I said Dad, you can't go sticking up signs without asking someone.' Carol, pouted, licked her lips and fluttered her eyes. 'You're very young to be a doctor. I get this pain in my....'

Emlyn scowled at Carol.

'I'm not a medical doctor. I'm a traffic hump doctor. Is there something in your eye?'

Carol stopped blinking. 'Hump doctor!'

'The secret of a good hump is the sub-strata and the type of tarmac. It's a very interesting subject.'

Emlyn and Carol looked spectacularly uninterested.

'The point is, it's got to come down; your sign, it's too big, doesn't comply with planning rules. I'm here to tell you to remove it or the council will issue an enforcement notice and take you to court.'

Emlyn considered what the young planning officer said and, after some moments to decide, agreed it was best to take the offending sign down.

Beryl was furious when she learned about the planning officer's threat. 'I'll sue the council,' she announced and stormed off.

'We'll need to paint a sign on the inside of the window,' said Emlyn. 'Can you think of anything?'

'Yea,' said Carol. 'A pig.'

133

Beryl phoned the council to complain about the threats impudent Dr Rees made. The nameless person she spoke to listened unsympathetically until Beryl started shouting when suddenly the line went dead. Beryl rang back insisting she be put through to someone senior and was passed on to a Mr Lewis. Mr Lewis sounded more reasonable and promised to come to the cafe to see her. 'I'll show them. They can't behave like little Hitlers,' announced Beryl putting the phone down.

Emlyn, who was responsible for feeding the pigs, was starting to worry. His daily trips to the feed merchant were getting expensive - very expensive. The piglets were growing but they were also eating like, well pigs. 'It's costing a fortune,' he said. 'They're eating us out of house and home.'

They were in the kitchen, discussing the problem, when there was a loud knock on the front door. Carol went to answer it and returned followed by a policeman.

'Beryl Jenkins?' He removed his helmet.

'Yes.' Beryl looked confused.

'I'm Constable Owen. I have reason to believe you've been moving pigs.'

'No,' said Beryl. 'You're quite mistaken.'

The policeman pressed on. 'Did you not purchase a pig from a farmer in Powys?'

'Yes.'

'Ah! So you admit it,' said Owen jubilantly. 'You have been moving pigs.'

'No. It wasn't pigs.' Beryl smirked. 'Only one pig was involved.'

The policeman sat down at the table and took out his notebook. 'I need to see your HS/MD.'

Beryl looked blank.

'Your Haulier Summary Movement Document.'

'Would you like a cup of tea officer?' said Emlyn.

'That's very kind of you Mr Jenkins. Two sugars. Mrs Jenkins, I'll need to see your CPHN and your movement notification. Did you notify through the EAML2 system or phone the MLCSL to notify?'

Emlyn busied himself with the kettle.

Carol texted *WEG Copper here 'bout pig. Mum in SHT*

WEG? asked William.

With Evil Grin. LOL

'Constable Owen, you come bursting in here asking me silly questions,' snapped Beryl. 'Spouting letters like a machinegun. Accusing me of I don't know what. Explain yourself.'

'Here's your tea,' said Emlyn.

'I need to see your CPHN your County Parish Holding Number.'

'I don't have one. Why should I?' demanded Beryl.

Owen scribbled in his notebook. 'Did you notify the movement by email or phone Meat and Livestock Commercial Services Limited to tell them you were moving the pig?'

'Don't be silly. Why should I do that?'

'It's the law Mrs Jenkins.'

'Would you like a piece of cake Constable Owen?' said Emlyn and placed a slice of Madeira in front of the policeman.

'Now you're being ridiculous.' Beryl glared at the policeman. 'Coming here with your CP whatnots and MLCs. I've no idea what you're talking about.' She sat, red faced, opposite the constable.

Frustrated by the suspects reply Constable Owen tried again. 'You are the registered owner of a pig that goes by the name of Enid? You've admitted you did transport the said pig from a farm in Powys to here?'

'No I didn't.'

'Mrs Jenkins lying won't help. I'm trying to get to the bottom of this. Are you registered as the pig keeper at DEFRA?'

OMG She's gonna thump the copper Texted Carol.

'No I'm not.'

'I know that one,' said Emlyn. 'The Department for the Eradication of Farming in Rural Areas.'

Constable Owen, frowned, shut his notebook and rubbed his hand across his forehead. 'I give up.' He stood and put his helmet on. 'Mrs Jenkins there are legal requirements you need to fulfil to keep pigs. I suggest you get registered quickly and sort yourself out before I have to come back again.'

Emlyn showed the policeman out. 'That was close,' he said on returning. 'He could have prosecuted you.'

'Don't be silly,' said Beryl. 'It wasn't me.'

'Who was it then?' asked Carol.

'Well, first of all it was your father who paid for Enid then the two of you put her in the car and who drove the car? Your father. I had nothing to do with it. I was going to tell Constable Owen that.'

'He seemed a nice chap,' said Emlyn. 'I think we'd better do as he said.' Emlyn cleared the table and suddenly exclaimed, 'Weeds.'

'Weeds?' chorused Beryl and Carol.

'For the pigs. We could feed them weeds.' Emlyn went on to explain how he would ask Mr Pugh, their neighbour, if the pigs could forage in Mr Pugh's wood. 'They would grub up weeds, hazelnuts, that sort of thing,' he said. 'That's what they do in the wild. It'll save us a fortune.'

'Yea. Call the cafe 'Pigs on Weed' and have a pig in the window with a spliff,' said Carol and laughed.

Beryl looked aghast. 'Pigs on Weed sounds very unappetising. What's a spliff?'

Mr Lewis, a plump, bespectacled, grey haired man wearing a dandruff flecked brown suit arrived at 2 o'clock the following afternoon. He looked around the cafe, sat at one of the tables without being asked and produced a folder from his briefcase. Beryl was ready and engaged him immediately. 'Are you Rees' superior? That young man needs proper training...' She watched him carefully remove the top of a fountain pen and start to write. 'Are you listening to me?'

Mr Lewis continued to write stopping only to wait for ink to dry and to turn the page of his notebook.

'That man needs to learn some manners. I demand to know what you are going to do about him.'

' Mrs Jenkins.' He put his pen down and looked at her over the top of his glasses. 'If you have a complaint about Dr Rees you should take it up with the planning department, not me.'

'Oh,' said Beryl, 'but that's why I summoned you here. Don't you work in the planning department?'

'No. I don't work in the planning department. I'm the council's Environmental Health Officer and I've been notified, by my colleagues, that you haven't registered your business. That, Mrs Jenkins, is a criminal offence punishable by a substantial fine and up to two years in prison.' Mr Lewis took his glasses off and polished them with a handkerchief.

Beryl sat down. 'Two years in prison.'

'This is a food establishment.' Mr Lewis studied his glasses and replaced them on his nose. 'It's subject to food hygiene inspections and has to be rated. It must be registered. I shall also require to see your Allergen Policy, all your Risk Assessments and copies of your Hazard Analysis. Have you prepared them?'

Beryl looked vacant.

Mr Lewis tutted, shook his head and made a note in his folder. 'I'd like to see your Food Hygiene Certificate. As the owner or manager it needs to be Level Three.'

Beryl shrugged.

'I see,' He said and wrote *Mrs Jenkins has no hygiene qualifications.*

Beryl followed the inspector into the kitchen.

'Some of this equipment needs replacing and the walls will have to be clad so they can be washed down before you can open.' Mr Lewis added more notes to his report. He tore a sheet from his pad and gave it to Beryl. 'This is a 28 day notice to comply.' He then produced a clutch of leaflets and handed them to her. 'These will explain what you have to do in more detail.'

Beryl watched the inspector leave, read the title of the first leaflet *E.Coli 0157 Cross Contamination Guidance* and buried her head in her hands.

Mr Pugh, a thin taciturn man whose eyes seemed too close together, as if he was permanently studying the end of his nose, didn't want to help. He was a principled man with one overriding principle; to do nothing for nothing. He wasn't interested in having pigs running around in his wood until, that is, Emlyn made him an offer he couldn't refuse.

'You can have one of the pigs as payment.'

The word payment and the prospect of a freezer full of free meat cheered him up considerably. 'I'll not be responsible for the animals and I don't want a runt,' he growled and the deal was done.

Emlyn was leading Enid along the road, with a bucket of feed, followed by a passel of boisterous piglets when a police car drew alongside and slowed.

Constable Owen wound down the window. 'Where are you going?'

Confident that all the legal niceties were in order, Emlyn smiled at the policeman. 'I'm taking Enid and her piglets to Mr Pugh's wood.'

'I'll need to see your pig walking licence.'

Emlyn had collected a considerable wad of paperwork for the pigs but - a pig walking licence. What was that? He shrugged and shook his head.

A car drew up behind the police car and piped. Constable Owen got out and waved the car past. Stopped by the policeman, Emlyn's momentum had gone. Enid's head was in the bucket and the piglets were milling about.

'Sorry. I've got to keep moving before she empties the bucket,' said Emlyn and set off again followed by Enid, her piglets and, bringing up the rear of the procession, Constable Owen.

Retired post mistress, Mrs Lloyd, stopped cleaning her windows to watch. Passengers on the 64 bus looked on amazed by the strange spectacle of a man with a bucket followed by a large sow, a line of piglets and a uniformed policemen completing the rustic scene.

They reached the wood and, having enticed Enid and her brood in, Emlyn and the constable leaned on the gate watching the pigs snuffle about.

'Do you like pork?' asked Emlyn.

'My mum does a lovely roast leg of pork with crackling. It's hard enough to crack your teeth. Lovely,' said Constable Owen. 'It's the salt she rubs on it and the stuffing well...'

Both men were salivating.

'Lots of gravy and crispy roast potatoes,' said Emlyn.

'You going to walk them back tonight?'

'Home for bed. It's a quiet road, only three hundred yards.'

Constable Owen knocked a twig under the gate with his foot. 'You haven't got a pig walking licence have you Mr Jenkins?'

Emlyn shook his head. 'Never heard of it. How do I get one?'

'You buy it from the APHA. They have to approve the route.' Owen saw the confusion on Emlyn face. 'The Animal and Plant Health Agency. But you don't pay the APHA for the licence.'

'You mean it's free. We get something for nothing. Fair play.'

'You pay the RPA; the Rural Payments Agency.'

Emlyn thought for a moment and then slowly said, 'Bloody Beryl and her daft ideas. It's an... L..O..B..'

'What?'

'IT'S A LOAD OF BOLLOCKS.'

Emlyn applied for a pig walking licence and, a few days later, a letter arrived from the Animal and Plant Health Agency saying a Miss Bevan would visit the following week to inspect the proposed pig walking route.

Miss Bevan, fresh faced, enthusiastic and newly appointed to her role, arrived wearing a business suit, patent leather shoes and an air of nervous importance. 'I've got a copy of the map you drew,' she said. 'I'm in a hurry. It's along the road so I won't need to change.' She produced a phone and took photographs from the road as Emlyn filled his bucket and coaxed Enid from her field. She stood back as he moved into the road.

'Would you mind?' said Emlyn and pointed, 'the gate.'

Miss Bevan leaned across the slimy grass to pull the gate shut leaving a black mark on her hand. She looked around for somewhere to wipe it on, bent down and cleaned it, as best as she could, on a tuft of grass.

Emlyn, meanwhile, was moving the pigs along the road. Miss Bevan hurried after them taking photographs as she went. Engrossed in collection photographic evidence of the route she didn't notice a piglet at her feet. Her, too shinny shoe, connected with the piglet. There was an ear piercing squeal. The piglet went in one direction. A shoe in another.

Enid spun around and, with maternal instinct and a surprising turn of speed for such a large animal, charged towards her piglet's attacker.

Miss Bevan fled, the piglet ran off squeaking and Emlyn dropped the bucket unsure of who to chase after.

He found Miss Bevan sitting in her car. 'It's all right. They're all safely in Mr Pugh's wood.'

Miss Bevan wound down her window. 'That animal's dangerous.'

'You kicked her piglet. What would you do if someone kicked your child?'

'I don't have any children... It was an accident.'

'Enid didn't know that.'

'What, that I haven't got children?'

'No. That it was an accident. Here,' said Emlyn passing a not so shinny shoe through the window.

'You won't tell anyone?'

'No,' said Emlyn.

Miss Bevan approved Emlyn's pig walking route and, having been assured no one would learn about her pig kicking, gave Emlyn a leaflet on African Swine Fever and hurried away to her next important appointment.

Each morning Emlyn would walk the pigs to the wood and, each evening, he would walk them home. His daily routine became an attraction.

Children, on their way to school, would stop to watch. People would hang out of car windows to take photographs and post them on Facebook. Soon Emlyn didn't need the bucket. Each morning Enid, eager to get to the wood, would run ahead followed by her squeaking offspring and at the end of the day she would lead the charge home to their warm cosy sty. Emlyn had to jog along to keep up with them.

The Facebook posts went viral. Instagram pictures of Emlyn's pigs with joke faces appeared. A video of him running after his herd was seen around the world. Emlyn was invited to become a non-executive director of an animal rescue on LinkedIn and a buxom lady who's suggestive name was Elsie-May made a saucy offer on Tinder. Twitter was flooded with porcine puns. The hashtag #PORKY trended with hundreds of re-tweets. The

143

Carmarthen Journal picked up the story. *Mr Jenkins' Homing Pigs* ran the headline. *Pigs on Weed* printed the Western Mail. Carol suggested the headline to the dishy young reporter sent to cover the story.

Emlyn Jenkins' fame spread. He appeared on television, was invited to talk at WI meetings and tell his 'how I walks with pigs' story at Rotary Club dinners.

'The cafe's ready,' announced Beryl during dinner one evening. 'The pigs are getting nice and fat. Emlyn tomorrow you'll take one to the slaughterhouse. We'll keep Enid. She'll have to have another litter.'

'I won't,' said Emlyn.

'What did you say?' Beryl glared at her husband.

'I said. I won't... The cafe's not ready. You haven't done anything the health inspector asked. Do you really want to spend two years in prison? None of my piglets are going for slaughter.'

'I'd come and visit you,' sniggered Carol.

'You said none of my pigs are going for slaughter,' said Beryl. 'Your Pigs! Why not?'

'You told Constable Owen I bought them and drove them home. So they're mine.' Emlyn pushed his plate away. 'Because they don't deserve it. That's why.'

'No I didn't. I said I was GOING to tell him.'

Carol snorted. 'Yea!.. You didn't say that about Winnie when she went to the knackers' yard.'

'She didn't go to the knackers' yard. Winnie went to auction,' said Emlyn quietly.

'Same bloody thing - and you,' Carol pointed at her mother. 'You kept the money; MY MONEY.'

'HOW DARE YOU TALK TO ME LIKE THAT.' Beryl stood up.

Carol grabbed her phone and stood, stony faced, staring at her mother.

'Sit down,' said Emlyn quietly.

Nobody moved.

'I said sit down; both of you,' he whispered. 'I've been talking to Mr Pugh. He likes the idea and we've agreed.'

'Agreed what?' asked Beryl. ' What have you agreed with Pugh without asking me first?'

'You haven't done anything about registering the cafe, have you or doing the food hygiene course? And there's another thing you seem to have forgotten; you don't like cooking.'

Beryl opened her mouth to say something but couldn't think of an answer. Emlyn was right. She hated cooking and to be honest, following Mr Lewis' visit, the dream of opening a cafe had become a nightmare.

'We're not going to open a cafe,' said Emlyn. 'We are going to open a pig petting farm. I've spoken to the authorities...'

'The authorities! What do you mean you've spoken to the authorities?'

'Shush woman.' Emlyn held up his hand. 'Stop interrupting. The APHA, the MLCSL and the Animal Health Office...'

'And DEF,' added Carol.

'DEF?'

'That other one.'

They looked vacantly as Carol.

'The one you said stops farming.'

'Yes and DEFRA. Thank you Carol. I forgot them.' Emlyn paused to collect his train of thought. 'They all say there's no problem provided we follow a few simple rules. The summer holidays are coming. Do you see? We can charge for people to come in.'

'How much can we charge?' asked Beryl.

Carol fiddled with her phone.

'What are you doing?' asked Emlyn.

'Nothing.'

Emlyn leaned across, took the phone and read aloud. '*OMG pig petting farm LOL ROFL NGL Wana' job?* What is this gibberish?'

Carol rolled her eyes. 'Oh my God. Don't you know anything?'

'That's no way to talk to your father.'

'OMG - Oh my God... I'm telling you what it means. It's to William... A pig petting farm, LOL - laugh out loud, ROFL - roll on floor laughing, NGL - not gonna lie, do you want a job?'

'I've decided,' declared Emlyn. 'NGL.' He grinned as Carol. 'We shall open on the first of August.'

The phone pinged; a reply from William. *Not a porky? OMG Yea DEF XXX*

15 I Blame Spud

A quick drink after work. That was the suggestion and why not? Spud said we all deserved a celebration and it's not often he puts his hand in his pocket.

We all call him Spud, the boss that is, but not to his face of course. Why? You might ask. It's really quite simple. He's a big Yorkshire-man with a nose that looks like it's been mashed and a pockmarked face that looks - well like it's chitting, and there's something else. His name is Edward King. I'm not sure who first called him Spud but it describes him to a tee.

Anyway, before I so rudely interrupted myself, back to the night in question.

It was a warm evening that warned of approaching thunderstorms, hot, energised. The sort of night that's charged, when you know something is going to happen. The pub was packed. Drinkers overflowed onto the pavement and, if I'm honest, I was enjoying myself. I sent a text to Janice, *Having a pint with Spud. Will get 6.45pm train. Love You.*

That was the plan but I didn't know then it was about to go horribly wrong.

Dinner's ready. Pork chop, apple sauce, mashed pots and veg, Replied Janice.

I'd never seen Spud socially and the difference in him was surprising. Was it the beer that changed this taciturn man? Spud normally spoke so slowly he seemed to be chewing each word, savouring its taste before reluctantly letting it escape from his mouth. 'Another?' he said and went to the bar.

I texted. *Make it two. Will get 7.45pm. Keep dinner warm.*

That night Spud was different. He was speaking excitedly, firing whole sentences like machine gun bullets, spraying the air with words. 'Of course yer 'avin another. Don't be such a pansy. Bloody 'ell. You Welshmen don't know how to enjoy yer selves.'

And that was it. You didn't argue with Spud. Who said, 'One is too many and two is never enough.'? Whoever it was, it wasn't Spud.

I texted Janice again. *Sorry 9.45pm train. Love Y.*

There's little pleasure in dwelling on the grizzly details of the evening, the moment when Colin dropped his trousers and mooned at a passing car or the girl from reception, the one with big teeth and eyes like gob stoppers, whose laugh - a kind of loud inhale followed by an explosion of snorts - got progressively louder.

I sent another text. *10.45pm train. Soz.*

By then Spud was doing Tommy Cooper impressions, big teeth was laughing almost continuously with tears running down her cheeks and Colin was attempting to sing 'Men of Harlech' to the karaoke machines while it played the music for 'Never Smile at a Crocodile'.

I did a mental count. Was it six or seven drinks? And Spud was ordering more. I had to get away, to escape the approaching wreck when the evening would crash and burn.

Beep. *Where are you?*

I fumbled with the buttons. *Walking to Stn.*

I'm going to bed. Came the reply.

Staff were locking the station up as I ran along the platform and jumped aboard the 11.45 train. I'd just made it.

I settled in a corner seat and tried to stay awake, to concentrate on getting off at my stop. Sleep, I knew, was dangerous.

Black countryside rattled past. Lightning lit the night sky. Droplets of water streaked along the window. The rain had started. What if there was no taxi at the station? I didn't relish the idea of a seven mile walk in pouring rain.

I texted Janice again. *At Stn 10mins Raining. Meet me-pls?*

Emerging from the station I was relieved to see the car. The rain was bouncing off the pavement as I dashed across and jumped in. 'Thanks for coming.'

There was no answer and then I noticed something odd. Janice wasn't in the car. I looked around. No sign of her. Nothing. My muddled mind didn't understand until I saw the keys in the ignition and everything made sense. She'd left the car for me. How considerate but what a stupid thing to do. Really! Some women have no sense. Anyone could have taken it.

I slid across to the driver's seat, started the engine and drove home, relieved to be out of the rain but, at the same time, cross and determined to tell Janice how silly she'd been.

It took me some time to find the right key for the front door. I turned the hall light on. 'I'm home.'

Silence. She must be asleep. I ambled upstairs to the bedroom. Janice wasn't there. She wasn't in the kitchen. I looked everywhere. By now I was really confused and I didn't know what to do so I did the only sensible thing. I went to bed.

I tossed and turned during the night, dreaming strange dreams, lightning, crashes of thunder, banging, a woman shouting. It was light when I slowly unglued my eye lids and peered at the clock. Five-thirty. There it was again, that noise from the dream. Someone was hammering on the front door and shouting. I went downstairs, opened it and there she was.

'Where've you been?' I said. 'I've been worried sick.'

Janice shoved me aside and marched to the kitchen leaving a trail of puddles through the hall.

'You look like a drowned hedgehog, and why are you wearing a nightie and slippers?'

'Because,' she turned to face me. 'I was in bed, reading when you messaged me. Do you know what time it was?'

I scratched my head.

'Ten minutes you said. Not much time to get to the station. It was past midnight. Didn't think anyone would see me. I just grabbed the car keys and went. Didn't even stop to go to the toilet.'

'But you weren't there - at the station.'

'I was.' She scowled at me. 'I yelled and you just drove off.'

'I didn't hear you. Where were you?'

'I was bursting. It was an emergency. There was no one about, so I nipped behind the hedge to have quick pee.' She rubbed her hair with the kitchen towel. 'I heard the car start, ran out as you were driving away. Seven miles, that's how far the station is. Did you know that?' She threw the towel at me. 'Seven bloody miles. I'm going to bed. Your dinner's in the oven.'

Janice did eventually forgive me but she says, if I ever go drinking with Spud again she'll mash me.

16 Revenge

'Not guilty,' said the foreman of the jury. Uproar followed as the prisoner walked from the dock a free man. Wealth had bought slick lawyers and expensive barristers who knew how to play the law. Three weeks of anguish, of listening to dreadful details, of seeing my wife weep, all for nothing. The trial at Swansea Crown Court was over. I watched Guy Roberts gloating, standing on the court steps full of self importance, a swaggering, cocky rock star. He posed for the cameras.

'The case should never have come to court,' declared his solicitor jubilantly. 'My client has been proven innocent.'

Roberts looked directly at me and smiled. In that second, a flood of emotion, of hatred like I'd never experienced before, overwhelmed me. I'm not a violent man but it was then, as he sneered contemptuously at the world, I, coward that I am, decided to do something I'd never done in my life - I decided to kill him.

The following morning I went to The Fisherman's Yarn looking for Petch, a man I knew only by reputation. The landlady, a stout woman with a broken nose watched, gimlet eyed as I approached the bar.

'A whisky. A large one. I'm looking for someone.'

'Who might that be?' She drained the optic and placed the glass on the bar. 'That's six pounds eighty.'

I handed her a ten pound note. 'Keep the change. His name's Petch. Has parachute regiment wings tattooed on his right arm.'

'You're not a copper. What you want him for?'

'I need his help.'

She studied me for a moment, shrugged and pointed to the lounge bar. 'He's in there.'

A big man, red faced with hands the size of dinner plates, was sat on the far side of the lounge. He was alone. A half empty beer glass was on the table in front of him. The dimly lit room was cold, uninviting. It smelt of rancid fat and stale alcohol. Banket seats lined the yellowing walls.

He didn't move as I crossed the room.

'Are you Petch?'

He looked up and I saw danger in his eyes. 'Do I know you?'

'No but I've been told you might help me.'

I placed the whisky glass on the table. 'I've a job for you. If you're interested.'

'A job... You'd employ me? I'm a soldier.' Petch emptied his beer glass and placed it upside-down on the table. '... I was a soldier.'

'I want to kill someone,' I said quietly.

'You want me to kill someone. Just like that. You come in here and tell me you want me to kill someone?' Petch picked up the whisky glass and drained it.

'No. I've got to do it but I don't know how.'

154

Petch sniffed and wiped his nose with his cuff. 'How do I know you're not a copper?'

'You don't,' I replied. 'But why would a policeman say he wants to kill someone?'

I waited while he digested my answer. Would he help or tell me to get lost? Laughter came from the public bar. I daren't move.

'Who is it? Who do your hate so much?'

'His name's Guy Roberts. He killed my daughter.'

'Roberts, the bloke who got off yesterday. It was on the news... So you're the father.'

I took my driving licence from my wallet and handed it to him. 'William Hurst. Her name was Christine. He can't get away with what he did.'

Petch studied my photograph and dropped the licence on the table. 'I can't help you.' I was disappointed but not surprised by his answer and, I will admit, almost relieved. Was his refusal to get involved a last chance to change my mind? I wanted revenge, to repay Roberts for what he'd done but at the same time I was afraid, not afraid of killing Roberts. He deserved to die. I was afraid of being caught. The idea of going to prison for murder, of what it would do to Karen, of the humiliation, frightened me. I'd been a fool to even thing of killing Roberts. I apologised to Petch for wasting his time and left.

The next day when we got back from taking fresh flowers to the cemetery I saw a note on the door mat. *Meet me. Seven o'clock Fisherman's Yarn,*

Petch. I screwed the note up and put it in my pocket. 'Karen, Are you going to WI this evening?'

'I don't think so. I can't face everyone. Why?'

'You should go. We can't sit in the house brooding for the rest of our lives. We've got to get out. I thought I'd go for a pint.'

'Bill you haven't been out for a drink since it happened.'

'You don't mind do you?'

Karen hugged me. 'I know how difficult it's been. It's hard for both of us. You go but, honestly, I can't deal with all the sympathy, the sad faces. I'll be alright. I'll find something on the television.'

Petch was smoking outside the Fisherman's Yarn when I arrived. He stubbed out the cigarette and finished his beer. 'It's busy inside. There's nowhere private to talk. Let's go for a walk in the park.' Petch walked quickly, frequently glancing about as if he was expecting someone to join us or spy on us.

'You said you wouldn't help so why are we meeting?' I asked.

'I needed to check you out. To make sure you were who you said you were.'

The confusion and fear I'd felt at our last meeting returned. I was hot from walking quickly and my heart was pounding. 'So you will help. Why did you change your mind?'

'I read the newspaper reports. Roberts is a scumbag but that's not the reason. I'm not doing it as a favour. I need money and you're going to pay.'

We stopped and sat on a bench seat.

'How d'you want to kill him?' Petch moved closer. 'A knife? Cut his throat?' He held his fingers to my neck. 'Strangle him? Poison? Do you want him to die slowly? To watch the horror on his face - see the pain - to enjoy the spectacle?'

'No.' I wiped perspiration and globules of spit from my face... 'I don't know.'

'Are you willing to go to prison?'

Getting caught, prison - The word formed a knot in my stomach.

'You've gone white. You afraid Mr Hurst?'

'Will you help me?'

'Twenty thousand pounds,' said Petch quietly. 'In cash, in advance.'

'I'll pay you half tomorrow and the rest when it's done, when Roberts is dead.' It was as if someone else had said the words, promising to pay this killer to help me, committing me to a path of action with no way back.

Karen looked surprised but didn't argue when I said I had to go away on business for a couple of days. I returned to Carmarthen the following morning.

Petch, shaved and looking presentable, was waiting at the side of the road. He threw a bag in the back and got into the car. 'You got the money?'

'It's on the back seat,' I said as I pulled away. Petch reached over and picked up a hessian bag, spilling bundles of notes as he yanked it into the front of the car.'

'Ten thousand pounds, as we agreed. Are you going to count it?'

'Do I need to?...' Petch pushed the bag into the foot-well. 'I trust you.'

'This is Tynant Manor where Roberts lives.' I handed Petch a photograph. 'It's near Llangollen.'

'Nice,' said Petch.

We drove to Llangollen and booked rooms in a tavern.

The landlord stood behind the bar and watched me sign the register.' Mr Parson and Mr Walsh. How long are you gents staying?'

'Two maybe three nights,' replied Petch and glanced at me.

The landlord passed us two keys. 'We're not busy so that's fine. Do you want to pay for two nights?'

I paid cash for the rooms and studied the beer pumps. 'I'm ready for a drink. Llangollen bitter, what's it like?'

The landlord pulled a taster into a spirit glass and gave it to me. 'It's a local craft beer. Quite strong. You can really taste the hops.'

The beer tasted fruity and refreshing. 'It's good. I'll have a pint. You having one?'

'No,' said Petch. 'Give me an orange squash. No ice.'

'Squash? Don't you want a beer?'

'I said no. Buy me a beer when we're done.'

We sat at a table and looked at my laptop.

'Go to Google Earth,' said Petch. 'You said he lives at Tynant Manor. Let's have a look.' I magnified the image.

'There might be a good place.' Petch pointed to a hedge lined field, at the bottom of the screen.

'Plenty of cover.' He held a beer mat against the scale and used it to estimate the distance to the house. 'About six hundred metres but is there a line of sight? Did you load the map like I told you?'

I nodded and clicked a link. An ordnance survey map appeared on the screen.

Petch used the cursor to draw a straight line between the hedge and the house. He read the numbers on the plot. 'I was right. Six hundred and forty metres and the house is twenty one metres lower than the field. We'll be hidden and able to retreat without being seen. There are no footpaths so we shouldn't be disturbed. We'll have a look tomorrow.'

'I'm going for another beer.' I picked up my empty glass. 'You sure you don't want one?'

'No,' said Petch, 'and you shouldn't either. We both need clear heads tomorrow.'

Petch had changed. He was focused, thinking ahead and the swagger was gone.

I put the empty glass down. 'Is Petch your real name?'

'No, it's Church.'

'Church! So where did Petch come from? It can't be your first name.'

 Petch shrugged. 'My first name's Peter, Peter Church - Petch - get it? It was my nickname in the army.'

I tried to imagine him as Peter. The name didn't fit.

The following morning was overcast and threatened rain. We dressed in dark walking clothes, drove to Tynant, parked a mile from the village and hiked across the fields to the hedge Petch had chosen on the map. We didn't speak and were careful not to be seen as we approached. Petch unpacked binoculars and a groundsheet from his rucksack, spread it out and we laid on the ground. Tynant Manor, gothic, large and rambling was in the valley below us.

'Now we wait and watch,' said Petch. He scanned the house with the binoculars and handed them to me. 'You have the first shift.'

I adjusted the focus and looked at the manor house. We had a perfect view. I could even see the furniture in the rooms. A security man, cradling a shotgun, was standing by wrought iron gates leading to a lane. A man was, raking the lawn, at the back of the house.

It was after four and Petch was watching, when the gardener left on a bicycle. A short while later the security man was relieved. At half past a black Mercedes approached along the lane. The gates opened. The vehicle drove to the front of the house and stopped. Two men got out of the car. One opened the rear door.

'He's there, Roberts, getting out of the car,' said Petch quietly. We watched Roberts go into the house. A light went on. He reappeared in an upstairs window.

'That must be his bedroom,' said Petch.

The curtains closed.

It was dark when we got back to the tavern.

160

'How many times have you fired a rifle?' Petch asked during dinner.

'I was in the Air Cadets. Did some shooting then.'

'You're telling me you haven't fired a rifle for more than twenty years?' Petch frowned. 'What weapon?'

'A .22 Martini Action. We used to shoot on a twenty-five yard range in the basement of the drill hall.'

'And you think that's the same as hitting a man at six hundred metres?'

The question hung in the air.

'You don't think I can do it, do you?'

'You'll miss. Then what?.. You won't get a second shot...' Petch was staring at me. 'Are you having second thoughts?'

'Yes... No. I mean... No. I'm not having second thoughts.'

'If this is going to work, I need to see you shoot. We've got to be sure. I'll think of something.'

We observed Tynant Manor for three days then, believing we knew enough about Roberts' routine and his security, we returned to Carmarthen.

Petch got out of the car and grabbed his bag from the back seat. 'I'll ring you when I have the rifle.' He turned and walked away.

Petch phoned the following day and told me to meet him at an old barn. 'It's remote,' he explained. 'No one will be about.'

161

The next morning I walked down a narrow, muddy track to a metal barn in a small wooded valley. A section of corrugated roof had collapsed and hung at a perilous angle. It moved, with every puff of wind, clanking against the side of the barn.

Petch was sitting on the seat of a rusting, long abandoned, tractor. He pointed to a gun bag on the ground.

I unzipped the bag, took out the weapon and held the gun up to look through the telescopic sight.

'Stop waving it about. It could be loaded,' snapped Petch.

I pointed the gun at the floor. 'It's a pellet gun.'

'That's right. A .22 air rifle.'

'Are you serious? I'm going to use an air gun.'

Petch climbed off the tractor and took the gun from me. 'No. I'm going to see you shoot with it.' He pointed to the end of the barn. 'See those little white targets on the corrugated wall. They're twenty-five metres away. I want to see you shoot. He gave the gun back to me and handed me a tin of pellets. 'Go on. Load it. Let's see if you can hit one.'

I broke open the gun and fumbled, dropping a pellet. I took another, pushed it into the breech, aimed and fired. The pellet hit the sheet metal with a ping.

'Missed,' said Petch. 'Try again.' The next shot also went wide.

I turned to look at Petch. 'What am I doing wrong?'

'Why are you pointing a weapon at me? Take your finger away from the trigger, put the safety on and point the gun at the ground. NOW,' ordered Petch. 'Rule one. Assume at all times your gun is loaded and ready to fire. Never, never point it at someone unless you intend to use it...' Petch walked to the target. 'You missed the target by a hundred millimetres. At six hundred and fifty metres you would be more than a metre wide. You've missed by nearly five feet.' He shook his head. 'Everything's wrong. Your breathing's wrong. The gun's going up and down like a see-saw. You're gripping it like a vice, trying to force your aim, and you have no balance. You're standing like John Wayne and snatching at the trigger like a cowboy.'

I knew, pointing the gun at Petch had been stupid and his dressing down had un-nerved me. I felt like a naughty child.

'Give me the gun.' Petch took the weapon. 'Let's start with your position. You won't be standing. The shot will be from a prone position.' He laid down and demonstrated. 'Your body needs to be at fifteen degrees from the line to the target. Like this. Here, you try.'

I laid down beside him and took the rifle.

'It needs to feel natural, as if the gun wants to point at the target. When you shut your eyes and open them again it should still be pointing in the same place. When you breathe the gun will rise and fall. Breathe steadily and squeeze the trigger slowly as you exhale and the cross hairs are on the target. Don't jerk or you will miss. Try it.'

I reloaded and fired.

'That's better. You hit an outer ring. Again.'

163

The lesson continued until Petch was satisfied. 'Five in the bull. A good grouping. I'll make a marksman out of you yet.'

We met again the following week in a wood. I followed Petch through the forest, up a steep bank, to a clearing overlooking the trees.

Petch took the gun bag from his shoulder and opened it. 'It's a superb weapon, A Bergara hunting rifle. You couldn't ask for anything better and these,' he produced a handful of bullets from a pocket, 'are Creedmoor shells. They're boringly accurate, capable of MoA accuracy.'

'MoA, what does that mean?'

'It means 'Minute of Accuracy'. They'll hit a one inch target at one hundred metres.' Petch was grinning. 'All we need now is a marksman who knows how to use them. To make it simple for you, I've set the scope for the distance you will be firing from. Just centre the sight on the target and shoot. Down there, can you see it?.' He pointed at a white square on a tree. 'That's Roberts. The range and elevation are right. Take your time and do exactly the same as you did with the air rifle. Keep your aim steady after you squeeze the trigger and remember, this gun has a recoil. Your shoulder will feel it.'

I loaded, took aim, waited until I was breathing out and squeezed the trigger. The rifle discharged with a loud crack. The noise was louder than I expected. I felt the kick, the energy of the weapon.

Its intoxicating authority. Here was power, the power of life or death. I grinned.

'Feels good doesn't it? A hit left side,' said Petch and lowered his binoculars. 'Try again.'

I fired more shots. Petch adjusted the telescopic sight, correcting the aim. I fired again and again, enjoying the thrill of each hit.

We walked down to examine the target.

Petch grinned. 'Well done. That's a difficult shot. You're ready. Look at this.' He examined the back of the tree. 'See the splinters. The bullets have ripped right through. Hit Roberts anywhere in the chest and the job's done. He won't get up.'

'Where did you get the rifle?' I asked. 'It's beautiful.'

'From a farmer. He boasted about going deer stalking with it. Loads of pictures on Facebook. Idiot even posted a picture of the gun safe he kept it in.' Petch ripped the cardboard target from the trunk of the tree.

'You stole it?'

'Course I stole it. What did you think? I'd ask to borrow it.' Petch slung the gun over his shoulder. 'The light's going. Let's get back.'

I slept badly that night. My mind was in turmoil, reliving, the trip to Tynant, the afternoon with Petch the power of the rifle, of life and death.

'Wake up,' shouted a voice. 'You're having a nightmare.'

I sat upright and wiped sweat from my eyes. The room was dark.

My wife was standing beside the bed. 'What were you dreaming about?'

'I don't know,' I mumbled and went to the bathroom. 'I can't explain. I tried to warn you.'

'You kept yelling, 'Get down, hide'. You nearly pushed me out of bed.'

I splashed cold water on my face. 'I'm sorry. I was trying to warn you. To save you.'

'To save me from what?'

'I don't know.' But I did know. In the dream I was looking through a telescopic sight. I could see a house clearly and beyond it the sea. 'Have you ever fired a rifle?' asked Petch. His words made no sense. It was the wrong house. My aim moved back to a window. 'Creedmoor bullets... Minute of Accuracy,' whispered Petch in my ear. 'All we need now is a marksman who knows how to use them.' I resisted, tried to hold the rifle away, but my arms wouldn't obey.

Petch was speaking again. 'The gun wants to point at the target.'

A woman, was moving in one of the rooms. I watched, helpless, as I slipped the safety catch off and put my finger on the trigger. I shouted, to warn her, 'GET DOWN, HIDE,' but she didn't hear. She walked to the window and looked straight at me.

'Squeeze the trigger,' ordered Petch. 'Do it now.'

Nausea overwhelmed me. I was aiming at my wife.

'Wake up,' shouted a voice.

I returned to the bedroom and feigned sleep but there was no escape from the vivid horror of my

166

dream or the nightmare thing I planned to do. I lay, on my side, watching my wife breathing gently as she slept.

Early rays of sunlight crept into the room. I got up, dressed quietly and went downstairs. The dream had scared me but the plan had been made. It was too late. I'd paid Petch and he would want the rest of his money. No, I had to finish the job and today, finally Roberts would get his justice. Karen was still sleeping peacefully when I left the house.

My heart thumped as I drove. I felt sick as I relived the dream. What did it mean? Why had I aimed the gun at Karen? A warning perhaps □ an excuse to turn around and go home - to forget everything. 'Roberts wasn't important,' I told myself. It wasn't the answer I wanted to hear. I imagined Christine and what he did. I don't remember much of the journey but suddenly I was there, at Tynant.

I crept along the edge of the field and laid in the mud by the hedge. Ripe ears of wheat swayed in the breeze, bright and golden. I looked back to check my retreat wasn't visible, unfastened the gun bag, slipped it off my shoulder and took out the rifle. Above me translucent green leaves shimmered in the sunlight, framed by a luminous blue sky. I felt frightened, excited, alive and more aware, that ever before, of everything around me. Somewhere to my left a wood pigeon 'cooed' in the trees. I eased the barrel through the hedge and scanned Tynant Manor through the telescopic sight. The house was quiet, a silent stage waiting for the final act. An engine noise distracted me; farm machinery. A combine harvester, working in the next field, was coming nearer. Would the driver, high in his cab, see me? I moved closer to the hedge. The noise grew louder then faded as the machine turned. An hour passed. The combine stopped. A tranquil quiet settled across the countryside, deceptive, unreal. I ate a chocolate bar, folded the wrapper neatly and stuffed it into my pocket. The sun was close to the horizon now. Roberts was late. Soon the light would fade.

A black Mercedes pulled up.

I got into position, aiming at the limousine, slipped the safety catch off and tried to relax, to make the gun want to point at the target.

The driver got out and opened the rear door.

'Move,' I muttered.

He stepped back as Roberts got out of the car.

I breathed out and slowly squeezed the trigger.

Roberts fell with a small puncture in his back.

Afterwards I ran. It was done. I threw the rifle in the river and switched on my mobile. It buzzed, a voice mail, a message from my wife. I wanted to ring her. To tell her, the evil bastard, who raped and strangled our little angel, was dead, that justice had been done but I knew I never could. It would forever be my dark secret.

I listened to the message from Karen. 'Why's your phone switched off? I've been trying to ring you for ages. The police have arrested a man. They said he's killed other girls. He's confessed. The verdict was right. Roberts didn't kill Christine. He was innocent.'

A Walk in the Woods

17 Ty Uchaf Rose

Mrs Wynn-Williams studied the man standing on the pavement; thirtyish, unshaven, tired and alone. He looked like a tramp; an unlikely house buyer, probably passing the time waiting for something, a bus perhaps, or for the food bank on the corner to open. But then he opened the door, came inside and waited sheepishly. She put down her nail file, straightened her jacket, patted her hair and stepped from behind her desk. 'Good morning. Are you looking for anything in particular?'

'You've got a house in window,' he mumbled looking at the floor.

'We've a lot of houses in the window. Rent or buy?'

'What?'

'Are you looking to rent or buy?'

'Buy. Ty Uchaf. It says forty thousand.'

Ty Uchaf, The Upper House, he was interested in it, maybe not a time waster after all; a chance to get rid of the albatross. Mrs Wynn-Williams switched on her charming face, selected a brochure and offered it to him. 'It needs some work but the location on the mountain is stunning. Would make a lovely holiday cottage.'

He ignored the outstretched hand. 'Why's it so cheap?' He looked up and met her gaze - piercing blue eyes demanding an answer.

What should she say? The truth, that no one who knew the house was interested, that it had been on her books for more than a year, that it was remote, that it was...

She patted her hair, stiff with lacquer. 'The owner's looking for a quick sale. There's a lot of interest,' she replied and beamed a cherry red smile. 'I can give you directions to view. Mr?'

'David Morgan. Yes I'd like that.'

David Morgan drove his battered Range Rover into the farmyard and turned off the engine. A dog was barking.

A farmer emerged from the house and came towards him. 'Quiet Russ,' he yelled.

The dog growled a final warning, cocked its leg against a tyre and slunk away.

'Am I going the right way for Ty Uchaf?'

'You are. Follow the track through the gate over there. It's a quarter of a mile further up the valley. You can't miss it. The track ends there. You thinking of buying it then?'

'I don't know. Maybe. Thanks,' said David and drove on.

The track was, narrow, overgrown and riddled with potholes. Branches clawed and scratched the Range Rover as it bounced along. A twisted ash tree screeched as it scraped against the roof. He stopped. Ahead, framed by an arch of branches, was Ty Uchaf.

David got out and surveyed the house, the collapsed slate roof, the ivy covered stone wall, voids where windows once hung. The building looked empty, soul-less; a remote, brooding ruin flanked by an oppressive tunnel.

Walking on, more came into view, a lean-to on one side, rough stone outbuildings, a cowshed and a rusting Dutch barn. A loose corrugated panel clanked against the metal frame. A gate, beside the barn, opened onto the mountain - brown and dry. Above it the sky, translucent, clear, clean, endless. Something moved in the house, a white shape, a sheep emerged in the doorway, looked at David and wandered off.

Turning around he looked back down the valley, toward the distant river and beyond it the town; civilisation - so near and yet so far.

Was it the view, the vast blue sky above, the mountain, the daunting challenge Ty Uchaf presented or perhaps his own grief the house was reflecting? David didn't know which but, as he stood there, he understood this remote derelict place was the escape, the retreat he was searching for.

A month later David moved a second hand caravan to Ty Uchaf. His offer of thirty-five thousand had been accepted. Ty Uchaf was his. He cut away overhanging branches and chopped back the hedges enough to tow the shabby caravan, which would be his temporary home and site office, up the track to the house.

The farmer, curious about his new neighbour, followed. 'You're going to live in it then?'

'While I do up the house.'

'My name's Evan, Evan Lewis.'

'David Morgan.' David opened a beer and handed it to the farmer. 'What do you know about the history of Ty Uchaf?'

Farmer Lewis made himself comfortable and began. The house, he said, had been empty for years, from before he was born. His father had told him about Mr Pritchard, a sour old shepherd, who lived alone at Ty Uchaf. The old man kept sheep on the mountain and didn't welcome visitors. Must have died more than sixty years ago. A young couple bought the place after that. Lewis remembered them, he used to play in the wood, but they only stayed a few months and then suddenly they left. No one knew where they went, he explained. 'One night they just packed up and disappeared. It's been empty ever since. Looks sad doesn't it?.. You married?'

David opened another can. 'I was three months ago.'

'Children?'

'A boy, Eddie. He's with his mother.'

They chatted until Lewis announced he had work to do. He called Russ to heel, thanked David for the beer and headed back down the track.

David watched the farmer until he vanished from view and reflected on what he'd said. Why had the young couple suddenly left? It seemed an odd story.

He was awake early the following morning and spent the day exploring the house, clearing rubbish and measuring rooms. He cut down an overgrown dog-rose by the front door. 'damn,' he said plucking a clutch of thorns from the palm of his hand. It was as if the plant was fighting back, not wanting to let go of the house. He sucked the spots of blood, wrapped the hand in a handkerchief and carried on working. He stacked old pieces of furniture outside and set them alight. That night he sat in the caravan, cleaned and dressed the gashes on his hand, and measured his progress. Making the house habitable was going to take time.

A week later the house was empty, a shell of a building with stone walls and rooms open to the sky. A rusting range stood in the kitchen, an iron bread oven in the corner of the fireplace and the floor, now swept, was covered in dirty brown clay tiles.

The sky was looking angry when David packed up work. Black clouds skidded across the sky. The air thick and clammy. A storm was coming. He shut the caravan door and settled down for the night. The wind whistled through a crack in the window and buffeted the caravan. David tried to sleep but strange noises kept waking him. Somewhere a branch shattered tearing itself away from the tree. Rain hammered on the roof. He dozed on and off sometimes dreaming and others half conscious. Suddenly, he sat up, fully awake, woken by a voice moaning pitifully. 'Noooo. Noooo!' It sounded like a man in pain but there was no one there. David was alone, listening to nothing but the howling wind and the metallic clank from the barn.

By morning the storm had blown itself out leaving a trail of destruction. A stream of water ran through the gate from the mountain. An ash tree by the track had been uprooted and what little remained of Ty Uchaf's roof was on the farmhouse floor.

David was up a ladder, stripping damaged corrugated sheets from the barn when an engine distracted him. Farmer Lewis was on a quad bike coming up the track with Russ perched on the back. 'Quite a storm. You all-right?' he called.

David climbed down. 'Barn's falling to pieces.'

'There's a delivery of building supplies in my yard. No way the articulated lorry was going to get up here. I'll bring the load up with the tractor later.'

'Thanks Evan.'

Evan Lewis was as good as his word and, supplied with timber and roofing materials, David set about rebuilding the roof. It was slow work but three weeks later he fitted the last slate. All Ty Uchaf needed now was windows and the house would be weatherproof.

David had finished his supper and was sketching a design for the kitchen. It had been a long day. His head nodded down towards the little table in the caravan. His eyes slowly closed as he drifted off. He fought the sleep but it overwhelmed him. Then, it was a bright day. David could feel the sun on his back. He was standing looking at the front of the house, across a carefully tended vegetable garden, rows of leeks, cabbages and potatoes. At one side a stand of runner beans and in the doorway a plump peasant woman wearing a wraparound pinafore. She had a pair of scissors in her hand and was cutting flowers from a rose bush. David's hand ached. He wanted to shout out, to warn her about the thorns, to show her the cuts on his palm but he didn't. He couldn't. He just stood watching her - afraid for her.

Then the woman looked straight at him, a frightened stare as if he was trespassing and shouldn't be there. She went in and slammed the door with a bang and, at that moment, David's head hit the caravan table.

Collecting post from the mailbox, down by the road the following morning, David's heart sank; he saw the crest on an envelope. It was a letter from his ex wife's lawyer. Expecting painful news he waited until he was back at the caravan to open it but the news wasn't bad, it was good - no, it was fantastic. The court had ordered Valerie, his ex, to deliver Eddie to visit David on one weekend a month including an overnight stay. David read the letter again.

She would bring Eddie next Saturday morning and return to collect him the following afternoon.

'YES.' David punched the air. There was a lot to do. Where would Eddie sleep? He had to be fed. What would they do? Fishing. Maybe a walk on the mountain. David's mind was racing. He had to clean the caravan, get some more bedding, go shopping, get a shave and a haircut. He'd show Valerie he could look after a ten year old. He started collecting empty bottles then sat down and wept; one night a month. She'd won again.

On Saturday morning a black BMW four wheel drive bumped slowly up the track. A man, David didn't recognise, was driving. Valerie was in the passenger seat and behind her was Eddie. The car stopped.

Eddie jumped out. 'Daddy,' he shouted running towards David.

They hugged.

'So this is where you're living. I didn't realise it was a bloody caravan. This is Carl.' She nodded to her male companion.

Carl, sour looking, built like a prop forward, offered a paw. Valerie's new man was a gorilla.

'The house hasn't got any windows,' said Valerie. 'Where are you living?'

'In the van,' said David. 'It's very cosy.'

Valerie pulled a face, went over to the caravan and stuck her head inside. 'Eddie, get back in the car. You're not staying.'

'What do you mean he's not staying?' David was still holding Eddie. 'One night. I'm entitled; the court order.'

'Bugger the court order. It's a shit hole. I'm not letting my son stay here. Carl put him in the car.'

Carl moved forward and took hold of Eddie's arm.

'Daddy,' shrieked Eddie.

'He's my son. Let go of him,' shouted David but Carl didn't let go. He snatched Eddie and dragged him back to the car.

'Daddy.'

David followed trying to stop them. The car door was open. He grabbed Carl's shoulder. Carl swung around and punched him, a swinging blow to the face. David staggered back.

Valerie shoved past him and got in. The car revved and set off down the track. David watched Eddie's face in the back window until he disappeared from view. He stumbled back to the caravan took a bottle from its hiding place under the sink and filled a glass.

It was dark when he woke. Someone, a woman in the distance, was sobbing. Her voice carried by the night air cried out, 'He's gone. You fool. Why did you let him go?' There was more shouting, a man. Was it a dream? He didn't know.

He woke again. Sunlight flooded the caravan.

Evan Lewis stood over him. 'By Damn, you look a mess.'

David sat up and fell back. 'She kept yelling 'He's gone. Why did you let him go?' Screaming it like a demented woman. Then a man shouted, 'We'll never see him again,' he muttered. 'I heard them in the night.'

David described the dream. 'I don't understand. Why would a woman in a dream be crying about Eddie?' Sure, he'd had a couple of drinks. Perhaps that was it? The booze. His addled mind was hallucinating, playing games, confusing reality from imagination? He remembered the dream with the woman in the doorway, the roses and his hand. It still hurt. 'Did the old shepherd have a wife?'

179

'Pritchard?' replied Evan. 'No. He lived alone.'

The woman in David's dream returned that night. It was raining. She was standing by the barn, eyes wide with fear. 'Help him,' she cried. David staggered toward the barn and clawed at the door but it wouldn't open. Then he woke, cold and wet, in his underclothes, standing beside the open barn. He was alone.

After breakfast David drove down to the village and parked by the church. The graveyard with its chamber tombs and drunken slate headstones was crowded and overgrown. Brambles covered names of the dead. Long grass tripped and pulled at his legs as he moved from grave to grave, searching, pulling back growth to read who lay within. A hazel tree coming through the middle of a burial. Arwen Hughes, Phyllis Reece, Jack Thomas, his wife Emily and three children - all in one grave. He moved on. Then, on a stone marker leaning against a crumbling brick wall near the back of the church, David found what he was searching for; Pritchard's final resting place. He read the carved headstone.

Meirion Pritchard
Ty Uchaf
4th September 1907 - 15th June 1957

But there was more. Above the old shepherd's name was an earlier carving of two more names.

Here lies
Alys Pritchard

Ty Uchaf
20th September 1910 - 15th June 1946
Beloved mother of
Alun Pritchard
26th April 1927 - 15th June 1945

Was Alys his wife? Was she the woman in David's dreams? So the old man had a family. He had a son. The burial looked unkempt, abandoned, unloved. Them David noticed something strange; the dates. He read the headstone again. They'd died in different years but always on the 15th June.

David wasn't sure why he did it but he returned to the churchyard with shears, a fork and a rake. He cut brambles back, cleared moss from the headstone and was on his knees, cutting grass around the grave, when he heard a voice.

'That's very good of you.' A clergyman was standing behind him. 'The churchyard is in a bit of a state. Are you a relative?'

David stood up. 'No. I've bought Ty Uchaf.'

The clergyman looked at David's grass stained trousers. 'It's good to see someone on their knees.' He grinned. 'You're welcome to do the rest. There's a strimmer in the shed.'

'Maybe another time.' For a second David wondered if he should tell the priest about his dreams. Father I've been...' He gathered up his tools. 'Did you know the family? I'd like to know more about them.'

'No. Never met them. I only came here a few years ago.' He looked at the dates. 'Mr Pritchard

181

died a long time ago. Go and talk to the retired post mistress, Mrs Owen. She's the village historian knows everything that happens.'

Mrs Owen, a tiny frail woman but sharp as a pin, lived in a sheltered bungalow at the end of the village. She listened as David explained how he was renovating a farmhouse. When he said it was Ty Uchaf she raised her eyebrows.

She made tea and carried a tray with her best china teapot and cups to the sitting room then went back to the kitchen, returning with a plate of Welsh cakes and a milk jug. 'Poor Mr Pritchard. I didn't know him well. I was only a young girl and, after it happened, I wasn't allowed to go anywhere near Ty Uchaf. Mam had forbidden it. I wouldn't have gone anyway; too frightened. You must have one Mr Morgan. I baked them this morning.'

'Why did she do that? What happened?'

'It's a sad place. Full of pain.' She nibbled a cake and placed it on her plate. 'Some said he was a spiteful, bitter old man.'

David tried to guess Mrs Owen's age; eighty perhaps older. 'He was only fifty. That isn't old.'

Mrs Owen dabbed a crumb with a finger and put it in her mouth. 'Mam told me he died of a broken heart. Would you like more tea?'

'Do you know what happened to his wife Alys and Alun?'

'I wasn't born then. No one ever talked about them. Of course I wanted to know but all Mam said

182

was, 'Let the dead rest in peace'. So I stopped asking.'

Mrs Owen paused and David saw her eyes were wet, glazing over. She was looking straight past him. He turned.

She was staring at a photograph of a young soldier on the sideboard. 'I'm sorry. What was I saying?'

'Your father? He's a handsome man.'

'Died before I was born. He's buried at Fontenay in France. It's a lovely cemetery. Beautiful. So peaceful. I'm glad I went.' She dabbed her eyes with a handkerchief. 'Sorry.'

David replaced his cup on the tray. 'I'm sorry Mrs Owen. I didn't mean to drag up painful memories.'

'No. You came to ask about Meirion Pritchard.' Mrs Owen straightened up in her chair and looked straight at David. 'I'm afraid I can't help you anymore.'

Driving back to Ty Uchaf, David felt bad. He'd upset Mrs Owen reminding her of her loss, the father she never knew. He thought of the father. A man who never knew his daughter. Did he know she existed? Had he gone to war unaware he was going to be a father? Perhaps he was lucky; dying not knowing the responsibility or the pain of being a father - or was he. David pulled into the White Hart Car Park and called Valerie.

It went to answer-phone, 'Leave a message.'

'Valerie. It's David. We've got to talk. To sort something out. I don't want to go to court again. Ring me.'

She returned the call almost immediately. 'I told you David. He's not staying in that stinking caravan.'

'Yes. I understand but I have a right to see Eddie. The court order.'

'I don't care. Sod the court order.' Her voice, loud and clear on the car speaker, attracted the attention of a passing couple.

They grinned at David and hurried on.

'What if I took him away and we stayed at a nice hotel?'

'I don't think so. You've had your chance.'

David wiped sweat from his forehead. 'What does that mean?'

'You know bloody well.'

'That's not fair. I've been off the booze for weeks...' he said angrily. He took a deep breath. 'For the love of God. Please Valerie, I'm begging you.' He could hear muffled voices.

Valerie was talking to someone; Carl.

'Where? Which hotel would you take him too?'

'I don't know.'

'Get a life David.' The line went dead.

David got out of the car, slammed the door and went into the pub.

The next four months was a time of frantic activity. There were new windows to fit, wiring, plastering, plumbing, a water supply to connect. David threw himself into the project with renewed vigour. Each night, he returned to the caravan. He still heard distant sounds, voices in the darkness, had strange dreams but they no longer frightened him. It was as if he had acknowledged the past and in return Ty Uchaf had accepted him. Working on the house was cathartic, an escape from the pain of losing Eddie - something to focus on - and, as the days passed, the grief faded.

Winter snow gave way to spring flowers, snowdrops then daffodils. Soon the wood below Ty Uchaf was carpetcd with bluebells. Summer came. Ewes nursing early lambs were grazing on the mountain. At last the house, although not yet finished, was habitable. David moved a bed upstairs and prepared to spend his first night under a slate roof. Walking from the caravan with a bowl of crockery he stopped by the front door. There were new shoots on the rose he'd so savagely cut back and he remembered how the bush had fought back stabbing him with thorns. He rubbed the callous on his hand, remembered the dream; the woman by the door and smiled, glad that the rose, wild though it now was, had survived. Life was returning to Ty Uchaf.

That evening the range cast a comforting glow across the kitchen as David finished eating. He added a log to the fire and left the door open enjoying the warmth. Shadows danced across the walls. The house felt solid, safe, comforting. He dozed, waking to find the fire had died down leaving red embers in the grate. A chill had taken hold of the kitchen. David closed the range door, to secure the fire and went outside to relieve himself. A new moon emerging from the east scattered pale silver light across the mountain. Standing in the cold he looked up at the clear night sky, Orion the hunter aiming steadily west, and, ahead of Orion, Cetus the sea monster fainter but still distinct. The sense of space and distance was overwhelming and at the same time reassuring. David felt good and proud of himself; he was sober. He returned indoors and climbed the stairs to bed.

David woke consumed by a terrible dread. He was soaked in sweat and afraid. Something awful had happened. He checked the time - half past two. The house was silent. A distant owl hooted □ a dream perhaps - everything was normal. He turned on his side and tried to sleep but it wouldn't come. Thoughts of Eddie crowded in. David longed to see him. The house was habitable. He hadn't had a drink for over a month. Valerie had no excuse to stop him seeing his son.

But, when David came downstairs, he found that everything wasn't normal. The rug, in front of the fire, lay crumpled against the wall. The wooden chair, he'd dozed in, was on its back. Broken crockery lay scattered across the floor. The kitchen was a mess. But how? The door was locked. He couldn't blame the drink; he hadn't had any. Then he remembered the dates on the headstone and today was the 15th June.

David wanted to find out what happened at Ty Uchaf, all those years ago, and he wanted to see Eddie.

He phoned his lawyer. 'I haven't seen my boy for six months.'

'I wrote to you in December,' said the lawyer. 'Valerie told the court you were permanently drunk and squatting in an old caravan. They cancelled your visiting rights... Why didn't you reply?'

'I wasn't in a good place,' mumbled David. 'But things are different now. I've stopped drinking and I'm living in the house. You've got to help me.'

'The court would take a lot of convincing particularly with your history. Leave it with me.'

David wasn't encouraged by the lawyer's reaction. He didn't seem interested in David's problem and unlikely to do any good. It was time to fight back, to make Valerie understand Eddie was his son as well. He had to confront her himself. The school, that was the answer. He'd meet her and speak to her, make her see reason, as she collected Eddie.

David checked the time. He had three hours to kill, time to do some research at the church.

The vicar was talking to a woman near the altar when David arrived. 'So the summer solstice service will start at eleven and we'll have the band. Excellent.' He looked at David. 'Mr Morgan. You're back again.'

'Summer solstice,' said David. 'Sounds like a pagan festival.'

The vicar smiled. 'It was but if it gets bums on pews I'm happy.'

'I'm wondering if I might look at the parish register.'

'Pritchard family?'

David nodded. He followed the vicar into the vestry. They examined the register together.

'Here it is,' said the vicar. 'Meirion Pritchard. Date of Death - 15th June 1957. Cause of Death - Suicide by hanging. Place of Death - Ty Uchaf Barn. Oh dear. That is sad.'

'So the old boy killed himself,' said David. 'How awful.'

They searched an older register and found the entry for Alys Pritchard. Date of Death - 15th June 1946. Cause of Death - Broken Heart. Place of Death Ty Uchaf.

'Broken heart. Is that a proper medical term?' asked David.

The vicar shrugged. 'Odd isn't it.'

Going back through the entries they discovered there was nothing recorded for Alun Pritchard, no record of death or burial.

'Perhaps he isn't here,' said the vicar. 'Have you thought of that?'

'But his name's on the headstone.'

'That's common enough. To add the names of loved ones when they aren't buried in the same grave.'

If Alun wasn't with his parents, where was he? It was a question David kept asking himself as he drove to confront Valerie.

Valerie was standing at the school gates a short distance from other parents. 'What are you doing here?'

'I want to see Eddie. Why are you wearing dark glasses?' David looked closer. He could see bruising around her left eye. 'What's happened to your face? Was it Carl? Did he hit you?'

'Daddy,' shouted Eddie and raced towards his father. They hugged.

'I've missed you boy.'

'I've missed you too.'

'Come on Eddie,' said Valerie. 'We need to get home.'

Eddie clung to David. 'I don't want to. You can't make me.'

She went to grab his hand.

Eddie wriggled away. 'No. No.'

Valerie was crying now. A black streak ran down her cheek. She removed her sunglasses and wiped a swollen, bloodshot eye, with a tissue.

David guided them to his car, sat her in the passenger seat and told Eddie to get in the back.

'No David. My car.'

'Never mind your car,' said David starting the engine. 'We can get it later.'

He'd been driving for several minutes when Valerie took out her phone and began to type. 'I'm texting Carl.'

'Don't.' David reached across and took the phone from her.

They drove on in silence until Valerie asked quietly, 'Where are we going?'

189

'Eddie, do you remember coming to see me when Carl dragged you away? I'm going to show you the house. If your mum agrees you'll be able to stay there with me. Would you like that?'

'Daddy I...'

'He can't stay with you. The court won't allow it.' Her words cut the air like a knife. No one spoke for the rest of the journey.

When they arrived at Ty Uchaf Valerie refused to get out of the car so David left her and took Eddie inside. They were talking in the kitchen when Valerie appeared in the doorway. 'I want to go home now.'

'Welcome to my home. Sit down Valerie,' said David. 'Eddie's been telling me how he's getting on at school.'

Valerie didn't move.

'Eddie wants to stay for a couple of days, don't you Eddie?'

Eddie looked anxiously at his mother.

'Have a look around Valerie. Go upstairs. The place is clean, warm and I promise you one thing. There isn't a single bottle in the house.'

'Can I mum, for the weekend - please?'

'Course you can Eddie. Can't he Valerie?' David stared at Valerie waiting, silently pleading for a reply.

'Two nights but you bring him back on Sunday afternoon.' She took off her glasses. 'Don't let me down, David or, I swear, it'll be the very last time.'

David and Eddie took Valerie to collect her car, pick up some things for Eddie and returned to Ty Uchaf.

It was after nine, they'd finished supper, when David's phone rang.

'Valerie. What's wrong?' David could hear loud music and laughter in the background.

'Nothing's wrong. I rang to see how Eddie is.'

'He's fine. We're playing Monopoly. Say hi to Mum.'

'Hi,' shouted Eddie.

'See you on Sunday.' David ended the call, declared Eddie the winner, and went upstairs to make Eddie's bed, leaving Eddie alone in the kitchen.

He sat watching the flames dancing in the grate. He'd never been by an open fire before and was fascinated by the swirling patterns appearing and vanishing. As Eddie sat alone, in the warm kitchen, a strange feeling took hold. He, could smell fresh bread and felt as if there was someone else in the kitchen, but he wasn't afraid. It was as if something nice was near, something that would protect him, love him almost. He looked around, at the dark corners of the room, and imagined he saw an old woman - or was it a shadow? He knew she wasn't real. How could she be? There was no one there. She smiled at him with her arms outstretched...

'You alright Eddie?' asked David. 'You look half asleep.'

Eddie told his father about the smiling woman. 'It was like she was trying to hug me.'

'The fire makes strange patterns. I see odd things sometimes,' explained David. 'You've had a long day. Time for bed young-man. Tomorrow we're going on an adventure.'

He didn't say anything to upset Eddie but his son's comments concerned David. Sure, he hadn't seemed afraid but who had he imagined he'd seen? Could the image be of Alys smiling at Alun - some strange physic throwback perhaps? Then there was the question of what happened to Alun. According to the headstone he died in 1945. The war, was that it? Was he a soldier?

David sat up late, his mind racing; Valerie's bruised face, Eddie's vision, Pritchard hanging in the barn, Alun, Alys's ghost - a confusion of emotions all competing for attention. He fetched a bottle of brandy, hidden under the sink, poured a tumbler full and sat staring at it. 'Where are you Alys? What do you want?' he whispered.

The slow, steady ticking clock was the only answer. Then he heard Eddie snoring, quietly, upstairs and in that moment he knew what to do. David picked up the brandy, poured it down the sink and opened his tablet. Searching the British Army Casualty Lists to begin with was easier than he'd expected. Alun's name, date of birth and date of death was all he needed. He learned, aged seventeen, Alun had enlisted in the 6th Battalion Royal Welch Fusiliers and in August 1944 parachuted into Southern France as part of the 2nd Parachute Brigade where he was seconded to Free French Forces and wounded at Toulon. He died in hospital and was buried at Mazargues War Cemetery, Marseilles.

'That's where your boy is, Alys. He's in France,' said David. He closed the tablet and got up. 'But you already knew that.'

A log disintegrated in the grate, flared and glowed bright red.

The next day David took Eddie fishing and they returned to Ty Uchaf with fresh trout. David showed Eddie how to gut and prepare the fish which they cooked on an open fire in the garden and ate with their hands.

'What do you think?'

'Fantastic,' said Eddie, wiping his chin. 'Can we go fishing again?'

'How did Mum get the black eye?'

Eddie didn't answer.

'I'm sorry. I shouldn't have asked.'

Eddie poked the fire with a stick. 'Can I stay?' He added more twigs to the flames.

'You can come again. If you want.'

'Yeah.'

'Next time I'll take you on the mountain. We'll explore the old lime kilns and the quarry where they filmed Doctor Who.'

'What here?'

'I'm not kidding. There were cyber men walking about on the mountain.'

Eddie was very quiet on Sunday as they drove back to Valerie's. They were nearly there when he suddenly said, 'She said it was an accident. She fell over but it wasn't true. They were arguing. I heard them. Carl shouted, called her a terrible name.' Tears ran down Eddie's cheeks. 'I don't want to live there. I want to live with you.'

David stopped the car. 'I know. I want you to live with me but it isn't that easy. I have to take you home or we'll be in trouble with the court.' He gave Eddie a hanky. 'Now dry your eyes. You've got school tomorrow. Give me a little time. I promise Eddie. I'll work something out.'

Carl was outside the house when they arrived. He waited until Eddie had said goodbye and gone inside then turned to David. 'If you ever pull a stunt like that again pestering Valerie I'll have you.'

'Where's Valerie?'

'She's in the house. Doesn't want to see you.' Carl opened the car door. 'Now shove off.'

'Bloody thug,' muttered David as he drove away. He reflected on the weekend. It had been wonderful. He'd never taken Eddie fishing before, never spent quality time with him before □ work had always been more important, deadlines to meet, a boss to please, a ladder to climb - and he'd been so stupid. He'd neglected his son and his wife, relationships sacrificed to his ambition, his foolishness and then there was the drink; compensation - relief from the pressure. At the time, he'd blamed Valerie for not supporting him, not understanding why he was working so hard. He'd thought she was being selfish. Looking back, the breakdown was inevitable. Why hadn't he seen it coming, stopped drinking, done something about it? He had to talk to

Valerie, like adults, to put things right. The lawyer wouldn't help but there had to be another way; a mediator perhaps - someone who was neutral, who would listen to his side.

David found Christine Franks, a Family Court Mediator, on the internet and emailed her. She replied the following morning suggesting a phone conversation. They talked. Her voice was confident, reassuring. She was a good listener, asking question, drawing out the issues. Franks understood what David wanted and promised she would contact Valerie to propose she act as a mediator. 'And,' she added, 'It was time that Eddie was asked what he wanted.'

Christine Franks' interest and her promise to help changed David. He was getting somewhere, someone was on his side. Ty Uchaf too had changed. Eddie's visit had filled the house with life. David wandered between the rooms, restless, excited, unable to focus. He had new enthusiasm and was working on finishing Ty Uchaf with renewed passion. He couldn't explain exactly why but the house felt different; warmer more homely. Coming into the kitchen one morning David was convinced he could smell fresh bread. On another occasion he was sure the chair by the fire had been moved. He never saw anything strange but he knew Alys was in the house. He could sense her presence, feel that she was near. When he slept he dreamt of how the house once was and how it could be again.

A week later an email arrived from Christine Franks. She'd been talking to Valerie and had good news. Valerie had said yes to a meeting.

It took a month to get Valerie to agree to let Eddie spend weekends with his father.

'Carl's gone,' said Eddie when he saw David. 'They had another argument and Mum told him to leave. She's got a new boyfriend, an electrician called Barry. He's nice.'

'That's good. I'm pleased for your mum,' said David.

The visits went well and the bond between father and son grew stronger as the months passed.

'We're going on a journey,' announced David. 'I've arranged it with your mother. She's said you can go.'

'Where to?' asked Eddie.

'To France. We'll fly from Bristol.'

On the way to the airport they stopped at the churchyard and planted a tiny rose cutting by Meirion and Alys' grave.

The flight was full. Landing in Marseilles they had to queue for a taxi and shared one with two old gentlemen who'd also been on the plane. The taxi took them to Mazargues War Cemetery. People were milling about reading epitaphs, waiting expectantly. A military band was playing in front of a crowd. They found Alun's grave where Eddie made a small hole in the dirt and pushed a sprig of rose into the ground. He stood up. 'Will it grow?'

'I think so,' said David. 'Do you know what today is?'

'Eleventh of November, Armistice day,' replied Eddie proudly. 'When we remember the war.'

At TyUchaf the following spring the bush by the front door was a mass of pink blooms. Elsewhere two tiny roses flowered, one in the village churchyard and a second in a far off war cemetery.

A Walk in the Woods

18 The Boy In The Picture

It smells funny, not very nice. It's my first visit. I'm six years old in a small room. Grandpa has brought me to see Aunty Peggy. She sits upright in an armchair beside the fireplace. The wooden sides of her chair are shelves filled with books. A tiny coal fire, surrounded by red bricks, burns in the centre of the grate. There are lots of ornaments, dogs and cats, on the shelf above the fire and a brown photograph in a big wooden frame hangs on the wall; a little baby, with no clothes on, lying on a sheepskin. A bare bottom sticks up and a face, rearing up like a tortoise's, looks back at me.

Aunty Peggy's eyes, black as the coal in the bucket, bore through me. She points at me with a crooked finger and nods. She scares me.

'He's a fine boy.' She smiles.

'What did you have for breakfast, Margedann?' asks Grandpa.

'Half a boiled egg with bread and butter. I shall eat the other half for lunch.'

A wisp of smoke escapes from the fire into the room. She jumps from the chair, seizes a poker and rams it into the fire, shattering a coal. Little blue flames spurt from the pieces. How small she is.

We don't stay long. She beckons as we leave. I move closer to the chair. Her arm reaches out. A bony hand grips my shoulder and draws me to her. I can smell her breath as she hugs me. She takes a little leather purse from the table behind her chair, opens it and takes out a coin. She presses a shiny half crown into my hand and folds my fingers around it.

'Grandpa, who was the baby in the picture?' I ask as we wait for the bus.

'That was Aunty Peggy's son, Perris. We don't talk about him.'

'Why?' I ask.

'It would make Aunty Peggy sad.'

'Is she my aunty?'

'She's really my aunty,' says Grandpa, 'but we all call her Aunty Peggy.'

'But you called her Dan? That's a boy's name.'

Grandpa pulls a face. 'No I called her Margedann. Her proper name is Margaret Ann Owen. Margedann is a nickname.'

'Margedann.' The name feels funny as I repeat it.

I'm ten. Aunty Peggy is in the same chair surrounded by her books. Perris looks down at me willing me to ask. He remains a mystery trapped in an old oak frame. It's a warm day but the little coal fire, surrounded by bricks, still burns. Margedann smiles at me.

I blush. 'That's a nice table,' I say to break the silence. I point to a little table, with twisty legs, beside her chair.

'William, my husband, made it,' she says. 'He made that too.' She turns and looks at a dresser behind her. 'Can you see the letters 'WO' at the top. William Owen. He carved them.'

I admire the dresser. 'It's very good. Was he a carpenter?'

'No. He was a school teacher. He made the dresser in his spare time and gave it to me on our wedding day.'

Grandpa arrives with two shopping bags. 'Be a good boy and fill Aunty's coal bucket,' he says. 'Then we must be off or we'll miss the bus.'

I take the bucket to the coal shed and fill it. I can't lift it and have to take some out.

'Come here,' she says as I return.

I know what's in her hand. It's worth a bony hug.

We are upstairs on the bus on the front seat. Grandpa always wants to sit on the front seat.

'Why does she keep his picture on the wall?' I ask.

'Perris?' says Grandpa, 'Because she loved him very much.'

A bridge is coming.

'Duck,' says Grandpa.

I pretend to duck.

He always says duck when there's a bridge.

'Is he dead?'

'Yes. It was a long time ago. It's a sad story,' says Grandpa. He smiles at me and winks. 'I'll buy you an ice cream at the shop but you must eat it before we get home and you mustn't tell Grandma.'

I proudly show Aunty Peggy the key-ring. 'It's a Vauxhall Viva. Cost me a hundred and twenty pounds. Would you like to come for a ride in it?' I ask.

She holds the keys in front of a large magnifying glass and inspects them. 'That would be lovely,' says Aunty Peggy but she doesn't move from her chair. 'How is Grandpa?'

'He's very unhappy. He won't come out of the house. Just sits there,' I reply. 'He loved Grandma very much.'

'Yes,' she says. 'I remember their wedding. It was Easter. Lambs were frolicking in the field behind the churchyard.' Her watery eyes sparkle. 'William was in uniform. He and I and Perris...' Her eyes glaze over. I watch a vein pulse beneath the gossamer white skin on the back of her hand.

The slow rhythmic tick of a clock punctuates the silence. 'Tick... tick... tick.'

I glance at the photograph above the hearth. Perris stares back, so young, so full of promise, of hope. There are brown blotches on the sheepskin. The sepia image is fading.

I don't know how to comfort an old woman pickled by time. I pick up her bucket and take it to the coal shed.

'Shall I make you a cup of tea before I go?' I say as I place the bucket by the fire.

She shakes her head.

'I'll come again soon Aunty Peggy.'

She holds out her hand. 'You're a fine boy,' she says and presses a fifty pence into mine.

I bend down and kiss her gently on the cheek.

Her embrace is vicelike, a bear-hug without end.

'This is Sue,' I say.

'Hello.' Susan smiles at Aunty Peggy and holds out her hand. The magnifying glass is held up to inspect the ring.

'You will come to the wedding?' says Susan.

'That would be lovely,' replies Aunty Peggy, but we know she won't.

She sends me to the kitchen to make tea. 'We have women's things to discuss,' she says.

We are driving away. 'What did you talk about?' I ask.

'She asked if we were going to have children. When I said yes, she said, 'You must have girls. Girls are better.' Why would she say that?'

'Aunty Peggy had a son, Perris,' I explain. 'She never talks about him. It was his picture is above the fireplace. I don't know what happened to him.'

'She seems so alone, just sitting there, as if she waiting for the end,' says Sue. 'What happened to her husband?'

'Grandpa told me, her husband, William died in the Second World War. He was killed in Italy. They never found his body.'

Our wedding is a spring one. Lambs skip and run in the field behind the church. Grandpa shuffles along slowly, with a stick, but he is there. We take cake to Aunty Peggy, show her the photographs and tell her our good news. Susan is expecting a baby.

'You must have a girl,' she says. 'Girls are better.'

203

I open the back door and go in. Grandpa follows. The house is cold. There's no fire in the grate. The chair is empty. A congealed tea cup sits next to the magnifying glass on the table, with barley twist legs, I admired as a boy. We move to the parlour; the room she never used.

Standing against the wall is a lid. I read the name, *Margaret Ann Owen 1879-1978.*

'She would have been one hundred next month,' says Grandpa. He wipes his eye.

Aunty Peggy is in her coffin. She is smaller than I remember - a wax doll with grotesque crimson lips, her bony hands clasped to her tummy, in silent prayer.

'He was very clever, a civil engineer,' says Grandpa. 'Perris went to South Africa to build a bridge. He came back in the 1920s during the great depression. There was no work. He committed suicide. Put his head in a gas oven. 1926 it was. She loved him but I don't think Aunty Peggy ever forgave him.'

He hands me his stick and slips a solitary rose between her fingers. 'She's left me the house but there's a bequest for you in her will.'

I imagine the argument with Sue. 'Not the picture?' I say.

'No,' says Grandpa. 'Not the picture. Aunty Peggy left you the little table with barley twist legs.'

19 The Man Who Never Was

'Don't give me stories. I don't want stories, I want reports.' It was old man Williams' favourite saying. Williams had been a newspaperman all his life. His job as editor of the *Carmarthenshire Mail* was, he believed, to explain to readers how the town worked, to give them the fact. Entertaining, interesting stories, quirky accounts like Dafydd's article about Mrs Owen's budgerigar attending town council meetings or Charlie's catchy headline 'I've been posting letters in the dog-poo box,'... not likely.

'Readers aren't interested in this rubbish. Write me a proper report,' he would shout and stab the air with his unlit pipe. Old man Williams' mission in life, it seemed, was to make the *Mail* the most boring newspaper imaginable and it was. The *Mail* was a dull-as-ditch-water daily rag.

'Silly old fart,' said Charlie. 'I'm sick of writing reports.'

'Yeah. He should be put out to grass,' said Dafydd and giggled.

'What?'

'I'm imagining him in a field, on all fours, with his pipe clenched between his teeth.'

The two young reporters were in The Star Inn. They often retreated to The Star, to get away from Williams, to contemplate why they were still working for a man who was, in their eyes, a fool.

'He never smokes it, the pipe,' said Dafydd. 'Just uses it as a pointer... Don't give me stories. I want reports,' he parroted and stabbed the air with an invisible pipe.

'It's his dummy.'

'Dafydd. You finished the leader for tomorrow?'

'Not quite. It's a bloody boring report on the state of the main road. 'Pot Hole Problem' that's the headline. Riveting stuff.'

'Arthur Jenkins, that's who we need,' said Charlie and winked.

'Arthur Jenkins, who's he when he's at home?'

'He isn't,' explained Charlie. 'Well not at home. In fact he isn't at all. He doesn't exist. I just made the name up.'

'If he doesn't exist, why do we need him?'

'To liven things up. Have a bit of fun. Let's put Arthur in tomorrow's paper.'

Dafydd frowned. 'We can't do that. It's unethical. Williams would go ballistic if he found out.'

The two friends smiled and raised their glasses. 'Don't give me stories. I want reports,' they chorused.

It was over that hurried lunchtime pint that Arthur Jenkins was born. He made his debut in Dafydd's front page leader the following morning when the article included these words. *'It's a disgrace,' says local resident Arthur Jenkins. 'The council should fill the holes in or something. I don't know what we pay our rates for.'*

If Charlie and Dafydd had been sensible Arthur would have quietly retired back into obscurity but it was not to be. The friends had got the bug. Arthur Jenkins would ride again.

A few days later Charlie was at ninety-nine year old Mrs Phillips' funeral. Mr Williams liked funerals. He wasn't interested in hearing about how sprightly old Mrs Phillips lived, about the glass of whisky she'd drunk for breakfast every day for sixty years - now there's a story. He didn't want to hear how wonderful she'd been or what marvellous things she'd achieved in her long life. He wanted names, specifically mourners' names. Williams believed readers loved to see their own name in the *Mail* and a full list of mourners was essential reading. A sure way to boost circulation.

Charlie stood outside the church, notebook in hand, asking the names of everyone entering the church - not an easy task. A light drizzle had started to fall and mourners, who were arriving in little groups, pushed past Charlie and into the church. Most didn't stop to give their names. After the service Charlie followed Mrs Phillips' cortege to the crematorium and copied the names on the wreaths. Even then Charlie knew he didn't have enough names.

The obituary appeared the next day and said, *'The mourners included Mrs Phillips' three children, Gladys Phillips, Jack Phillips and Phyllis Green...'* It went on listing other names, *'... and Arthur Jenkins...'* but the list didn't stop there.

Charlie was on a roll and had decided to make Mr Williams happy by adding more names; names he created from a mixture pinched from a telephone directory.

'That was a bit dangerous, wasn't it?' said Dafydd. 'What if the family say something or complain?'

Charlie shrugged. 'You try standing in the rain asking people what their names are. Of course I made them up. Old man Williams wanted a report of all the names. What else could I do?' He paused to reflect on Dafydd's comment. 'Nah. They won't complain. They'll be delighted that the old girl was so popular. All these people, they don't even know, coming to her funeral. What's to complain about?'

Where else might the phantom Arthur appear? Williams made Dafydd rewrite his piece on the Town Centre Safety meeting saying, 'I don't like your headline 'Safety Meeting Ends in Accident',' but he said nothing about the quote Dafydd included from Health and Safety expert A.J. Jenkins.

And so it went on with dear old Arthur a regular in the *Mail,* on the sports page, in news reports and magazine pieces. Dafydd even worked an Arthur into the daily cartoon strip. Astonishingly the editor never seemed to notice the odd regularity with which Arthur Jenkins was appearing in his paper until, that is, Charlie wrote the letter; a letter that would seal Arthur's fate.

'Only two letters this week,' announced old man Williams. He picked up the first and poked it with his pipe. 'Unprintable rubbish.' Into the bin it went. 'This one's about the stink from the sewage works.

We can use it. Charlie, I need some more letters to fill the page. Get to work.'

There was nothing unusual about the old man's order. *Mail* readers were so few in number and apathetic that few letters came to the *Mail's* offices. As a result Charlie and Dafydd regularly supplemented them by becoming Miffed from Manordeilo, Glad from Gwynfe or Confused from Capel Dewi to pen suitable letters to the editor.

The letter that led to dear Arthur's demise was a glowing tribute to the journalistic skill and editorial integrity of the paper signed, of course, by Arthur Jenkins. Although Charlie wrote the letter he didn't give it to old man Williams. It was safer, he thought, to leave it in the post tray to make it look like a real reader's letter. And that is what he did.

Old man Williams was delighted. 'Have you seen this,' he crowed holding it aloft. 'It's our letter of the week. Dafydd, go and see Mr Jenkins, pay him and get a photo.'

Letter of the week. When the lucky contributor was paid ten pounds and had their picture in the paper. Charlie hadn't thought of that.

Fortunately Dafydd had an idea.

The letter and a photo of Arthur Jenkins appeared in the following week's edition of the paper. Of course it wasn't really Arthur Jenkins' picture. It was a photograph of Dafydd's Uncle Stanley. Stanley didn't know he'd pictorially impersonated Arthur Jenkins since he lived in Ruthin and was unlikely to ever see the *Mail* or for that matter to see the ten pounds Dafydd, thoughtfully, shared with Charlie.

It had been a close call and both agreed it was time to say goodbye to Arthur but the pair couldn't resist one final outing for the old boy. The obituary was Charlie's idea. They'd send him off in style and so they did.

'Prominent local resident Arthur J. Jenkins, 73, has died at his home after a short illness.

'He was a retired civil engineer and a keen supporter of Llandovery Rugby Club who lived in Carmarthen since moving here 30 years ago from his native Wrexham. The mourners were.....'

Old man Williams was delighted with the mourners' list. At last, so it was hoped, Arthur was at peace but it wasn't so.

The following week a reporter from the *Wrexham Tribune* rang the *Mail* and asked for more details about Arthur Jenkins. For some obscure reason his editor had seen the obituary and wanted to do a follow up story. The job was passed to Charlie to respond who, always willing to help another journalist with the truth, embellished Arthur's background and emailed a reply.

That is how the life of Arthur J. Jenkins, a man who never existed, was celebrated in two newspapers.

20 Promises

'Send them a letter,' said Glenys. It seemed a good idea. Geraint took up his fountain pen and started to write on the Basildon Bond notepaper he'd been given last Christmas.

To Mr Jenkins - Managing Director, Crystal Double Glazing, Transparent House, Swansea. Dear Sir. Geraint put the pen down. 'Do you think I'm being fair?'

'The salesman promised, didn't he?' replied Glenys. 'I was here. I heard him say it.'

'Yes but Mr Jenkins will be cross.'

'That's not your fault. Maurice promised. He should be cross with Phyllis not you.'

Glenys was right. The salesman had made a lot of promises. Geraint remembered the evening the rep from Crystal Double Glazing came. He'd not really wanted new windows. The old ones were still perfectly clear, hardly worn out at all. The only reason he'd said Maurice could come was the girl on the phone sounded so nice.

'It's a free service,' she'd said.

'Are you quite sure?' Geraint had asked.

'Oh yes. It won't cost you a penny,' she'd explained.

The salesman, Maurice Black, was a short, tubby man whose belly hung over his trouser belt. The suit he wore was creased and there were stains which looked like tomato soup on his tie. 'Geraint, can I call you Geraint?' he said making himself comfortable on the settee. 'Pleased to meet you.' He

211

opened the sample case on the cushion beside him, looked around the room and smiled. 'What a lovely picture.' He pointed at the photograph of Geraint's mum on the sideboard.

Glenys' head had appeared around the door. 'I've cleaned the kitchen. Shall I do the bathroom next?'

'Ah. The good lady of the house,' said Maurice. 'You don't want to be cleaning bathrooms. You'll want to see what I can do for you. Come and join us.' He motioned to the empty chair. 'And you are?'

'Glenys.'

'Glenys, that's a lovely name.'

'Before you start. You're girl on the phone said this won't cost me a penny.'

'That's right Geraint.' Maurice smiled reassuringly at Glenys. 'It's a totally free survey.'

Then Maurice went to work. He described how terrible the old windows were, explaining how the heat escaped and cold came in. He took a little plastic window frame from his case. 'It's UPVC brilliant white. Never needs painting.' He produced a lock and passed it to Geraint. 'Five levers. Safe as houses.'

'What?' said Geraint.

'Safe as houses. This lock is burglar proof.'

'Oh,' said Geraint and handed the lock back.

Maurice took a tape measure. 'I'll start with this window. I like your curtains. They're lovely.'

'Are you sure, Maurice?' Geraint asked. 'You haven't told me any fibs?'

Maurice put his hand over the tomato stain and looked offended. 'Geraint, on my word of honour. I've never told a lie in my life. Not once.'

'Not even a little one?'

'Certainly not.' He paused. 'Except when I tried to wash the cat in the toilet. But I was only seven.'

The honesty of Maurice's reply and the admission he'd once tried to bath a cat in a toilet was, for Geraint, the decider. Maurice was a man he could trust. Forget the crumpled suit, the way he'd spread across the settee like a bloated whale or the soup stained tie. Maurice Black was a man of integrity, an upstanding pillar of the community, a man Geraint could do business with.

It was then that Glenys stood up. 'I've got to go. Jack'll be wanting his dinner.'

'Hang on,' Maurice said. 'I need you both to sign. Who's Jack?'

'My husband. Who'd you thing?' Glenys said and left.

'I thought she was your wife.'

'No,' Geraint replied as he signed the paperwork. The new windows were fitted two weeks later.

That was a year ago. Geraint's very pleased with his new windows. Pleased he'd believed the promises Maurice had made. The house was lovely and warm and, just as Maurice promised, the frames were still brilliant white. Maurice had been right about the locks too. Geraint hadn't been burgled once. Geraint was satisfied he'd made the right decision; he'd believed Maurice. The rep from Crystal Double Glazing had told the truth.

'It can't go on,' said Glenys. 'The woman's a pest. She won't leave you alone. I still think you should send them the letter.'

'You're right,' said Geraint and picked up his pen. He scribbled out *Dear Sir* and Wrote;

Dear Mr Jenkins,

I am writing to thank you for the excellent new windows your company has fitted. Your representative, a fine fellow called Maurice, did a wonderful job explaining how they would work and I must say every word was true. Not only that but I must congratulate you on the way your fitters worked. They only drank sixty one cups of tea and their Trojan bladder control is a wonder.

There is however one thing which I feel I must draw to your attention. I'm sure it's a genuine error, easily corrected. Don't get me wrong, I'm pleased that your company, in particular a lady called Phyllis, is keeping in touch but I cannot understand why she keeps writing to me saying I must pay you some money. When I spoke to her on the telephone last Tuesday she said I was supposed to pay you for the windows. There has clearly been a misunderstanding and she is obviously mistaken.

Will you please have a quiet word with her; don't be too harsh. But please tell her to stop ringing me up and writing to me. If she doesn't understand I suggest you get Maurice to explain. He's very good at explaining things.

You see, Maurice promised I would not have to pay for the windows. I remember his words clearly and Glenys heard them as well. She was there and although Maurice thought she was my wife, she isn't. I'm sure Maurice is now clear on that point. Getting back to the main issue it's really quite simple. Maurice said - and these were his exact words, 'Geraint don't worry. I promise you the new windows will pay for themselves inside a year.'

If they haven't done so, it's hardly my fault.
Yours sincerely
Geraint Reece.

Geraint showed the letter to Glenys. 'What do you think?'

'They can't argue with that,' said Glenys.

'I'll post it straight away,' said Geraint and then, with a flourish, he added a post-script.

P.S. Maurice particularly liked my curtains. If he wants I can tell him where I bought them from. I'm sure they will still have some the same.

A Walk in the Woods

21 The Curse of Nant Gwrtheyrn

Taken from Welsh Legends and Myths
80 Myths and Legends from across Wales

Gwrtheyrn was a king who lived in Kent during the 5th Century. He was a timid man and his kingdom was weak. He employed mercenaries from Saxony to fight his enemies and paid them with gold. The Saxons, led by the brutal warrior Hengist, drove off Gwrtheyrn's foes. King Gwrtheyrn was pleased and gave Hengist the Isle of Thanet as a reward. The Saxons bought their families to Kent and settled on the fertile island. Before long, they started to take more land. Seeing the danger he had invited into his kingdom, Gwrtheyrn negotiated a wedding to protect his throne. He asked for the hand of Alys, the beautiful daughter of Hengist, the Saxon leader. Hengist agreed to the match and a great feast was prepared with Saxons and Britons sitting together. Suddenly, as one, the Saxons jumped up, drew their daggers and stabbed the Britons beside them. Gwrtheyrn had been tricked. He escaped and ran for his life, accompanied by Druid priests.

The king and his priests travelled far across the land looking for a remote part of Britain where the evil Hengist would never find them. After years of searching, they found a small valley, hidden behind a mountain on a remote peninsula. The land could be ploughed and there were fish in the sea. King Gwrtheryn had found his refuge and the little party settled in the valley. They built houses and soon a thriving village was established, a village that was so remote that it should never be discovered.

One hundred years later, three Christian monks found a tiny track leading down a steep mountain and followed it to the valley below. Near the sea, they found a village with a pagan church. The monks told the villagers to build a Catholic church but the people refused. They threw stones at the monks and drove them away. The retreating monks stopped on the track, high above the village and each monk cursed the tiny hamlet below them.

'The ground in this valley is unholy. No man shall be buried here,' yelled the first monk.

'The men of Nant Gwrtheyrn shall never marry the women of Nant Gwrtheyrn,' cried the second monk.

'Your village is doomed and will be ruined three times. The third time it falls will be forever,' bellowed the third monk. The people in the valley heard the curses and laughed at the monks.

'Words cannot hurt us,' they said. The following day the men of the village took their boats into the bay to fish. A violent storm blew up and overturned the boats, drowning the men. The bodies disappeared into the sea. With no men, the women had no choice but to leave the village and start new lives. Nant Gwrtheyrn became a deserted ruin.

As the years passed, people began to return to the valley to farm, but strange accidents happened to the men. Some fell into the sea and disappeared beneath the waves. Others vanished into the forest, never to be seen again. Slowly, the graveyard filled with headstones carved with the names of their widows. Wary of the curses, the people dared not wed each other. The men travelled away from the village to find their wives and bring them back to the valley. Small farms were started but they were so far from any market and the track out of the valley was so steep that the farmers struggled to make a living. Eventually, people gave up and drifted away until there were only three farms left at Nant Gwrtheyrn called 'Ty Hen', 'Ty Canol' and 'Ty Uchaf'.

Rhys Maredydd lived at Ty Uchaf with his sister Angharad. They were orphans. Their father had been consumed in a terrible fire that had destroyed the winter hay. Their mother had died of a broken heart. The orphans had a cousin, Meinir who lived with her father at Ty Hen. The three children were friends and would play together when their jobs were done. As the youngsters grew older, Rhys and his cousin, Meinir fell in love. They wandered, hand in hand, on Mount Eifl above the farms. A great oak tree stood on the mountain where they would sit and plan their lives together, sheltered by the giant branches. When Rhys asked Meinir for her hand in marriage, she willingly agreed and the happy couple ran down the mountain to seek her father's permission.

'You cannot marry Rhys,' said her father.

'But we love each other,' cried Meinir.

'Rhys is your cousin. You cannot marry your neighbour. Remember the curse,' said her father. Tears ran down Meinir's face as her father spoke and his heart melted. He relented and embraced the young lovers, agreeing they could wed. Plans were made for the wedding. It was agreed they would wed far away from Nant Gwrthyren, at the church of Clynnog Fawr. Surely the curse would not hurt them there.

The morning of the wedding arrived. It was a fine summers day. Rhys dressed in his Sunday clothes and walked across the fields to Meinir's farm. Her father stood in the doorway, solemnly refusing entry. Eventually, to the merriment of the gathering wedding guests, Meinir's father grinned and stood aside. Rhys went inside to find his bride. Searching for the bride on the wedding morning is an ancient custom and Rhys went from room to room happily calling for Meinir to reveal herself but she did not appear. Meinir, eager to make Rhys work to find her, had slipped away to hide, long before her betrothed had arrived.

Enjoying the game, Rhys searched the barn and the cow sheds but they were empty. Meinir had vanished. He called her name but there was no answer. The wedding guests cheered and encouraged Rhys as he went from field to field looking for his bride. The morning passed and the sun beat down. Rhys grew hot in his wedding suit. He was no longer enjoying searching for Meinir. He called again. Still there was no answer.

'Perhaps she has gone to Clynnog Fawr and is waiting for you at the church,' said the wedding guests.

Rhys set off along the track, leading up the mountain towards Clynnog Fawr. The wedding guests followed behind as quickly as they could. But Meinir was not waiting at the church. Rhys turned and ran back towards Nant Gwrtheyrn desperate to find his bride. Meinir's father, weary from the long walk to the church, borrowed a horse and galloped after Rhys. The two men searched the farm again but could not find Meinir. The dark came but they did not stop. They cut torches and scoured the mountain through the night, calling for Meinir to reveal herself.

Rhys and Meinir's father continued to search as the months passed. Then one night Meinir's father did not return from the search. He was never seen again. Rhys was alone in the valley.

The corn went uncut and the cows grew wild as Rhys searched. Summer turned to winter but he would not stop. Each day Rhys would walk for miles called out, 'Meinir, Meinir where are you?' Each night he would sit huddled under the great oak tree on the mountain and cry softly, 'Meinir, Meinir where are you?'

Thirty years passed then, one night as Rhys sat shivering under the great tree, storm clouds gathered on the mountain. A flash of lightening struck the tree, splitting it in two. A hideous cry echoed across the valley for, in the flash of light, Meinir's hiding place had been revealed. There, wedged in the hollow trunk of the tree, stood the twisted skeleton of a young woman. All that was left of the wedding dress, that was once so pure and white, were a few grey rags hanging from the bones. Rhys was found next morning lying dead beneath the tree, with Menir's corpse in his arms.

The curse of Nant Gwrtheyrn had left the valley desolate and empty for the second time. It would be another 200 years before Nant Gwrtheyrn became ruined for the third and final time.

Other books by Graham Watkins

Most are available as eBooks, in paperback and as audio books.

Fiction
The Iron Masters
A White Man's War
The Sicilian Defence
The Enemy Within
Supernatural Stories
Welsh Legends and Myths - Eighty Myths and Legends from across Wales.
The Turnings of the Years - A collection of short stories from Llandovery Writer's Group of which Graham is a member.

Non Fiction
The Welsh Folly Book
Walking With Welsh Legends (Five Volumes)

Business
Exit Strategy
Birth of a Salesman
How to Sell Ice to Eskimos.
The Art of the Book Fair

You can learn more about Graham's latest writing and download free copies of some of his work from his website at **www.grahamwatkins.info**

Printed in Great Britain
by Amazon